Heinemann Short Stories
Two

Other Places, Other Worlds

Poetry Anthologies edited by Rhodri Jones

Themes Series
Men and Beasts
Conflict

Preludes Series
Families
Work and Play
Weathers
Five Senses

New English

A complete secondary English course by Rhodri Jones
New English First
New English Second
New English Third
New English Fourth (to C.S.E.)
A New English Course (to 'O' level)
An ABC of English Teaching
a teachers' handbook with examples taken from New English

Heinemann Short Stories
Two

Other Places, Other Worlds

Selected and edited by Rhodri Jones
Headmaster of John Kelly Boys' High School, Brent

Heinemann Educational Books
LONDON

Heinemann Educational Books Ltd
22 Bedford Square, London WC1B 3HH
LONDON   EDINBURGH   MELBOURNE   AUCKLAND
HONG KONG   SINGAPORE   KUALA LUMPUR   NEW DELHI
IBADAN   NAIROBI   JOHANNESBURG
PORTSMOUTH (NH)   KINGSTON

Cover design and photography by Chris Gilbert

First published 1980

Reprinted 1981, 1982, 1985

British Library Cataloguing in Publication Data

Heinemann short stories.
  Book 2: Other places, other worlds
  1. Short stories, English
  I. Jones, Rhodri
  823′.9′1FS   PR1309.S5

  ISBN 0–435–13491–4

Printed and bound in Hong Kong by
Dah Hua Company Ltd

Contents

Acknowledgements

The editor and publishers wish to thank the following for permission to reproduce copyright material:
Hamish Hamilton for 'The Best Day of My Easter Holidays' from *Black Faces White Faces* by Jane Gardam; Winant, Towers Ltd for 'Varlaam and Tripp' by Leon Garfield from *Miscellany Two* ed. Edward Blishen (OUP); Hart-Davis MacGibbon and A. D. Peters for 'The Fog Horn' from *The Golden Apples of the Sun* by Ray Bradbury; A. D. Peters and Paul Reynolds Inc. for 'The Mouse' by Howard Fast from *Zoo 2000* ed. Jane Yolen (Gollancz).

Illustrations

Introduction

The short stories in this collection are intended primarily to be read for entertainment and pleasure. They should appeal particularly to pupils in the second (or first) year of the secondary school.

They deal with other places and other worlds. These include other countries a long distance away, journeys into the past, supernatural and ghostly experiences, and adventures into the future. It is by reading about other worlds such as these that we can extend our own understanding of the world in which we live today. Reading and considering how writers give shape to their ideas and experiences and use words to make them more effective can help you to appreciate more the skills of the writer.

It can also help you when you come to write your own stories. There are notes and suggestions on each story at the end of this volume to guide you. If you enjoy a story by a particular writer, try to read more stories or novels by him or her: suggestions for titles to look for are given at the end.

The Best Day of My Easter Holidays

JANE GARDAM

The best day of my Easter holidays was the day we met Jolly Jackson. This year we went to Jamaica for our holidays because my father was working there and so we spent all his fees although it was still expensive and we didn't get any rake-off. When I told all the American people in our hotel we were there on my father's fees they thought it was very funny and said things to my father like 'I hear you're travelling light, bud,' and slapped him over the back in a way that puzzled him and made him angry.

The people in our hotel were all very, very rich. One was so rich he got paralysed, the beach-boy told me. Like Midas one side of him got turned to gold. He dribbled. The only one not rich was a vicar. He had gone there to a conference. My mother met him in the sea and they talked up to their knees. 'How lucky we are,' said the vicar in a HUGE American accent, 'in this so glorious country, enjoying the gifts of God. It is Eden itself.' Then he shouted 'FLAMING HADES' and fell flat on his stomach in the sea because he had been stung by a sea-egg. 'Help, help,' called my mother and everyone came running off the beach and dragged the vicar up the sand – blood everywhere. 'Ammonia!' cried someone. 'Only thing for a sea-egg is to pee on it,' said the beach-raker. 'Git gone,' said the beach-boy and my mother said, 'Come along now Ned dear, it's time we set off for Duns River Falls.' The other women turned away, too and only the men were left standing around the vicar who had five black spikes sticking out of his foot and was rolling about in agony. 'They never do no permanent harm, ma'am,' said the beach-boy to my mother, 'just pain and anguish for a day,' and he was laughing like anything – well, like a Jamaican and they laugh a great deal. I don't know if they did try peeing on the vicar or if they did if it was one or

3

all of them. I kept thinking of the whole crowd standing round and peeing on the vicar and I laughed like a Jamaican all the way to Duns River Falls until my parents said, 'Shut up or there'll be trouble.'

Duns River Falls are some waterfalls that drop into the sea. I had expected them about as high as a tower but they were only about as high as my father. Also they had built a road over them and kiosks etc., and ticket offices and I was fed up because I had wanted to stay on the beach.

My mother said, 'Well, now we're here –' and we began to park the car when a huge man came dancing along the road in pink and blue clothes and a straw hat and opened the door and shook hands with my father. 'Hullo Daddy,' he shouted, 'an' how are you today?' (Everyone starts 'An' how are you today.') 'Now then Daddy, outs you get and in the back. I gonna sit with Mummy.'

Now my father is a man who is very important at home and nobody tells him what to do. In Jamaica he doesn't wear his black suit and stiff collar or his gold half-glasses, but even in an orange shirt and a straw hat you can tell he is very important. Oh yes man. But when this great big man told him to get out and sit in the back he got out and sat in the back, and my mother's eyes went large and wide. 'Stop for nobody and dat's advice,' they had said in our hotel, 'Jamaica is a very inflammatory place. Yes sir.' Well this man held out the biggest hand I've ever seen, pink on the front, and said, 'My name's Jolly Jackson and what's yours?'

My father said, 'Hum. Hum. Ahem,' but my mother said, 'Mrs Egerton,' and held out her hand and I sprang up and down and said, 'My name's Ned, man,' and my father said, 'That will do.'

'This boy talks Jamaican, yes sir,' said Jolly Jackson, 'and now I gonna take you to see the wonderful Public Gardens followed by a tour of the surrounding countryside where you will find growing, pineapples, coffee beans, tea, avocado, coconuts and every single thing. Every fruit in all the world grow in Jamaica. Jamaica is the best country in the world and the sun is always shining.'

5

At that moment it began to rain in the most tremendous torrents and as our car was going up a hill which was probably once part of the waterfall and going about the same sort of angle, great waves began to come rushing down on us and the car spluttered and stopped and then turned sideways and began to be washed away.

'This is one of the famous Jamaican rainstorms,' said Jolly Jackson. 'The rain in Jamaica is the best in the world. It is very necessary rain. It rushes over the ground and disappears into the sea. In a minute it will be gone.'

We sat there for about half an hour and the rain hit the road like ten million bullets and went up from it in steam and the trees above dripped it back. Waves washed round our sideways wheels and my mother said, 'What happens if a car comes the other way?'

'Don't worry,' said Jolly Jackson, 'everything stop in a Jamaica rainstorm,' and then a huge great petrol tanker with all its lights on came tearing round the corner and down the hill towards us, screeched its brakes and skidded into the side of the road and fell into a ditch.

'Here comes the sun now,' said Jolly Jackson in a hasty voice, 'away we go,' and he got the car going and turned up the hill again and off before the driver of the petrol tanker had got the door open and got a look at us.

He was right and the sun came out and everything shone and steamed. When we got to the Public Gardens Jolly Jackson put his foot on the accelerator and roared through, past the ticket office. He was out and had all of us out in about a quarter of a second and all of us off down a path before my mother could even mop up her face.

'This here is the famous Jamaica red tree,' he said. 'This here is oleander, that there is the ban-yan tree only fifty year old, big as a mountain. That there is a waterfall. Now this boy and Mummy are gonna stand in the waterfall and have a photo.' He took the camera from round my father's neck, undid it and went click, click. Sometimes he turned the camera towards himself and went click, click and my father said, 'I say, look here –'

6

'Now,' he said, 'you will take a photograph of me,' and he stood inside a very dark trellis tunnel full of great big pale green lilies like long bells hanging, and stretched up and smelled one, arching his very long back, and a big white smile on his face. He stood there for a very long time even though my mother said 'It's in the dark.' In the end she said, 'Oh well,' and went click and then Jolly Jackson moved on.

I've never seen my parents go so fast. He simply ran up and down paths, in and out of groves and places, pointing things out, picking things – sometimes great huge branches of things. 'Take it, take it. Plenty more. Jamaica can grow everything.' Once he stopped dead and we all crashed into his back. He gathered us all together and said, 'Look now, just there. That is the true Jamaica humming bird,' and there of course was a humming bird with its lovely curly tail. It was sipping from a rosy flower. There are thousands of them at our hotel all round our table at lunch every single day. We didn't even notice them much after the first week, but now we all said 'Ooooooooooh.' Jolly Jackson somehow made you say 'Ooooooooooh.' Yes man.

Well, before my mother had seen half she wanted to he shovelled us into the car again and we stormed the barricades like James Bond or something and were off up a terribly narrow stony road with little Jamaican chicken-hut houses on each side in the trees and ladies doing their washing with lovely pink and yellow handkerchiefs on their heads, but we went so fast we couldn't get more than glimpses. My father said, leaning forward and tapping Jolly Jackson's shoulder, 'I think I should just mention that the car is only insured for myself,' and Jolly Jackson said, 'Now don't you worry Daddy, I been driving ten years. I fully qualified Private Guide and never an accident yet.' Just then a police car came rocketing round the corner and got into a tangle with our front bumper which fell off. 'Never mind,' said Jolly Jackson, 'these are my friends,' and everybody got out. There were three police men and two police women and they all laughed and laughed and shook hands with Jolly Jackson and Jolly Jackson introduced us. 'This is Daddy,' he said. 'A very important man in business from London, England, this is Ned and this is Mummy who is just at home.' This annoyed my mother who does a lot of writing work at home and gives speeches on how women are as important as men.

Well, we picked up the bumper and Jolly Jackson tried to put it in the boot and then threw it away under a banana tree. Then we went to see a lot of his aunts, cousins, great aunts, grandmothers and mother. They were all very nice and gathered round the car and told us about all their daughters who were all matrons in hospitals in London. Jolly Jackson's mother said that his sister was matron of several hospitals in London. 'That right,' said Jolly Jackson, 'my sister called Polly Jackson. I Jolly Jackson. She Polly Jackson. You go back to London and ask for Polly Jackson. She'll be there.'

My mother said to my father, 'I don't believe all this is happening.'

At one chicken-house place a whole lot of children gathered round who all seemed to be relations. One of them put his tongue out at me and said 'White face', but Jolly Jackson hit him. My father, after we'd waited simply ages gave some dollars round and we went on. Once we went up a very steep road and stopped to see coffee growing by the road and a woman came out of the trees, very pretty, with a baby with a sore leg. The leg had gone yellow, orange and purple all round the cut. She had cut it on a bottle last week, the mother said. The baby was hot and crying and my mother said, 'That child has a temperature, he needs penicillin,' (very fierce) and the mother of the baby drew back with a cold look and said, 'No Missis, I put on coconut oil. You think me Jamaican monkey.' A bad look passed between them. The woman said 'white face' and my father said, 'Oh come now' and handed more dollars.

'Do you think things are going to change in Jamaica?' my father asked Jolly Jackson as we went tearing on after this and he said, still in the same happy voice, 'Oh yes, man. Ninety thousand soldiers.' Actually he might have said, 'Nine thousand soldiers,' or 'Nineteen thousand soldiers' but it sounded like 'Ninety thousand soldiers,' and after that we were all quiet for a bit.

8

We seemed somehow after a very long time to get back to the same place, I don't know how. But it was terribly hot in the car and we didn't have any idea where we were. Then we saw the petrol tanker in the ditch and crowds and crowds trying to get it out and everybody smiling. Jolly Jackson's police friends were there and a lot of his other friends and we all got out again to shake hands, and we bought a pineapple for one dollar thirty which made my mother say, 'Fortnum and Mason!' Jolly Jackson introduced us to hundreds of his friends. Afterwards we went back towards the Falls again and we nearly hit another car and the driver leaned out and shouted a lot of queer language at us ending in Jackson. 'Is he your friend, too?' my mother asked, and Jolly Jackson said, 'No, I know him but he is not my friend.'

'Now, we all go in the Falls,' he said when we got to the parking place. 'All take off your clothes and we walk up the Falls, five hundred feet of pure Jamaican waterfall. Perfectly safe. Nobody never falls in, never.'

'NO,' said my father and gave him six dollars.

'Seven,' said Jolly Jackson, and my father gave him seven dollars, and we went off to look at the Falls by ourselves, my mother saying things like, 'Quite ridiculous. You are an utter fool, James. Daylight robbery,' and my father saying it was worth it just to be still alive.

Somehow going up the Falls was very dull though, without Jolly Jackson and we didn't stay long. Everyone looked very white and ugly and touristy and quiet. My mother even said as we left, and went to the car again, 'I suppose seven dollars was *enough*, James? He really did us rather well I suppose. We did *see* a lot. It took two hours.' But my father said 'Pah! Enough! Look!' and we saw Jolly Jackson by the car park all alone and dancing in the road.

I said I wanted to go and say goodbye to him again but they said, no. I said it wouldn't take long but they said, no dear, come along. 'Come along,' they said. 'Let's go back to the beach, let's see what's happened to the poor old vicar.' But that – the silly vicar and the man all paralysed with gold – didn't interest me any more. All that interested me was Jolly

Jackson and I watched him and watched him, so beautiful, out of the back window of the car, getting smaller and smaller. And he waved and waved to me as he danced and danced. He danced and danced not moving his feet but with all his body and his lovely smiling face. He was dancing and dancing and dancing and dancing in the very middle of the big main road.

That was the best day of my Easter holidays.

(B— Egerton. Rubbish. See me.)

The Loaded Dog

HENRY LAWSON

Dave Regan, Jim Bently, and Andy Page were sinking a shaft at Stony Creek in search of a rich gold quartz reef which was supposed to exist in the vicinity. There is always a rich reef supposed to exist in the vicinity; the only questions are whether it is ten feet or hundreds beneath the surface, and in which direction. They had struck some pretty solid rock, also water which kept them bailing. They used the old-fashioned blasting-powder and time-fuse. They'd make a sausage or cartridge of blasting-powder in a skin of strong calico or canvas, the mouth sewn and bound round the end of the fuse; they'd dip the cartridge in melted tallow to make it watertight, get the drill-hole as dry as possible, drop in the cartridge with some dry dust, and wad and ram with stiff clay and broken brick. Then they'd light the fuse and get out of the hole and wait. The result was usually an ugly pot-hole in the bottom of the shaft and half a barrow-load of broken rock.

There was plenty of fish in the creek, fresh-water bream, cod, cat-fish, and tailers. The party were fond of fish, and Andy and Dave of fishing. Andy would fish for three hours at a stretch if encouraged by a nibble or a bite now and then – say once in twenty minutes. The butcher was always willing to give meat in exchange for fish when they caught more than they could eat; but now it was winter, and these fish wouldn't bite. However, the creek was low, just a chain of muddy water-holes, from the hole with a few bucketfuls in it to the sizeable pool with an average depth of six or seven feet, and they could get fish by bailing out the smaller holes or muddying up the water in the larger ones till the fish rose to the surface. There was the cat-fish, with spikes growing out of the sides of its head, and if you got pricked you'd know it, as Dave said. Andy took off his boots, tucked up his trousers, and went into

a hole one day to stir up the mud with his feet, and he knew it. Dave scooped one out with his hand and got pricked, and he knew it too; his arm swelled, and the pain throbbed up into his shoulder, and down into his stomach, too, he said, like a toothache he had once, and kept him awake for two nights – only the toothache pain had a 'burred edge', Dave said.

Dave got an idea.

'Why not blow the fish up in the big waterhole with a cartridge?' he said. 'I'll try it.'

He thought the thing out and Andy Page worked it out. Andy usually put Dave's theories into practice if they were practicable, or bore the blame for the failure and chaffing of his mates if they weren't.

He made a cartridge about three times the size of those they used in the rock. Jim Bently said it was big enough to blow the bottom out of the river. The inner skin was of stout calico; Andy stuck the end of a six-foot piece of fuse well down in the powder and bound the mouth of the bag firmly to it with whipcord. The idea was to sink the cartridge in the water with the open end of the fuse attached to a float on the surface, ready for lighting. Andy dipped the cartridge in melted bees-wax to make it watertight. 'We'll have to leave it some time before we light it,' said Dave, 'to give the fish time to get over their scare when we put it in, and come nosing round again; so we'll want it well watertight.'

Round the cartridge Andy, at Dave's suggestion, bound a strip of sail canvas – that they used for making water-bags – to increase the force of the explosion, and round that he pasted layers of stiff brown paper – on the plan of the sort of fireworks we called 'gun-crackers'. He let the paper dry in the sun, then he sewed a covering of two thicknesses of canvas over it, and bound the thing from end to end with stout fishing-line. Dave's schemes were elaborate, and he often worked his inventions out to nothing. The cartridge was rigid and solid enough now – a formidable bomb; but Andy and Dave wanted to be sure. Andy sewed on another layer of canvas, dipped the cartridge in melted tallow, twisted a length of fencing-wire round it as an afterthought, dipped it in tallow again, and stood it carefully against a tent-peg, where he'd knew where to find it, and wound the fuse loosely round it. Then he went to the camp-fire to try some potatoes which were boiling in their jackets in a billy, and to see about frying some chops for dinner. Dave and Jim were at work in the claim that morning.

They had a big black young retriever dog – or rather an overgrown pup, a big, foolish, four-footed mate, who was always slobbering round them and lashing their legs with his heavy tail that swung round like a stockwhip. Most of his head was usually a red, idiotic slobbering grin of appreciation of his own silliness. He seemed to take life, the world, his two-legged mates, and his own instinct as a huge joke. He'd retrieve anything; he carted back most of the camp rubbish that Andy threw away. They had a cat that died in hot weather, and Andy threw it a good distance away in the scrub; and early one morning the dog found the cat, after it had been dead a week or so, and carried it back to camp, and laid it just inside the tent-flaps, where it could best make its presence known when the mates should rise and begin to sniff suspiciously in the sickly smothering atmosphere of the summer sunrise. He used to retrieve them when they went in swimming; he'd jump in after them, and scratch their naked bodies with his paws. They loved him for his good-heartedness and his foolishness, but when they wished to enjoy a swim they had to tie him up in camp.

He watched Andy with great interest all the morning making the cartridge, and hindered him considerably, trying to help; but about noon he went off to the claim to see how Dave and Jim were getting on, and to come home to dinner with them. Andy saw them coming, and put a panful of mutton-chops on the fire. Andy was cook today; Dave and Jim stood with their backs to the fire, as bushmen do in all weathers, waiting till dinner should be ready. The retriever went nosing round after something he seemed to have missed.

Andy's brain still worked on the cartridge; his eye was caught by the glare of an empty kerosene-tin lying in the bushes, and it struck him that it wouldn't be a bad idea to sink the cartridge packed with clay, sand, or stones in the tin, to

14

increase the force of the explosion. He may have been all out, from a scientific point of view, but the notion looked all right to him. Jim Bently, by the way, wasn't interested in their 'damned silliness'. Andy noticed an empty treacle-tin – the sort with the little tin neck or spout soldered on to the top for the convenience of pouring out the treacle – and it struck him that this would have made the best kind of cartridge-case: he would only have had to pour in the powder, stick the fuse in through the neck, and cork and seal it with bees-wax. He was turning to suggest this to Dave, when Dave glanced over his shoulder to see how the chops were doing – and bolted. He explained afterwards that he thought he heard the pan spluttering extra, and looked to see if the chops were burning. Jim Bently looked behind and bolted after Dave. Andy stood stock-still, staring after them.

'Run, Andy! Run!' they shouted back at him. 'Run! Look behind you, you fool!' Andy turned slowly and looked, and there, close behind him, was the retriever with the cartridge in his mouth – wedged into his broadest and silliest grin. And that wasn't all. The dog had come round the fire to Andy, and the loose end of the fuse had trailed and waggled over the burning sticks into the blaze; Andy had slit and nicked the firing end of the fuse well, and now it was hissing and spitting properly.

Andy's legs started with a jolt; his legs started before his brain did, and he made after Dave and Jim. And the dog followed Andy.

Dave and Jim were good runners – Jim the best – for a short distance; Andy was slow and heavy, but he had the strength and the wind and could last. The dog capered round him, delighted as a dog could be to find his mates, as he thought, on for a frolic. Dave and Jim kept shouting back, 'Don't foller us! Don't foller us, you coloured fool!' But Andy kept on, no matter how they dodged. They could never explain, any more than the dog, why they followed each other, but so they ran, Dave keeping in Jim's track in all its turnings, Andy after Dave, and the dog circling round Andy – the live fuse swishing in all directions and hissing and spluttering and stinking. Jim yelling to Dave not to follow him, Dave shouting to Andy to go in another direction – to 'spread out', and Andy roaring at the dog to go home. Then Andy's brain began to work, stimulated by the crisis: he tried to get a running kick at the dog, but the dog dodged; he snatched up sticks and stones and threw them at the dog and ran on again. The retriever saw that he'd made a mistake about Andy, and left him and bounded after Dave. Dave, who had the presence of mind to think that the fuse's time wasn't up yet, made a dive and a grab for the dog, caught him by the tail, and as he swung round snatched the cartridge out of his mouth and flung it as far as he could; the dog immediately bounded after it and retrieved it. Dave roared and cursed at the dog, who, seeing that Dave was offended, left him and went after Jim, who was well ahead. Jim swung to a sapling and went up it like a native bear; it was a young sapling, and Jim couldn't safely get more than ten or twelve feet from the ground. The dog laid the cartridge, as carefully as if it were a kitten, at the foot of the sapling, and capered and leaped and whooped joyously round under Jim. The big pup reckoned that this was part of the lark – he was all right now – it was Jim who was out for a spree. The fuse sounded as if it were going a mile a minute. Jim tried to climb higher and the sapling bent and cracked. Jim fell on his feet and ran. The dog swooped on the cartridge and followed. It all took but a very few moments. Jim ran to a digger's hole, about ten feet deep, and dropped down into it – landing on soft mud – and was safe. The dog grinned sardonically down on him, over the edge, for a moment, as if he thought it would be a good lark to drop the cartridge down on Jim.

'Go away, Tommy,' said Jim feebly, 'go away.'

The dog bounded off after Dave, who was the only one in sight now; Andy had dropped behind a log, where he lay flat on his face, having suddenly remembered a picture of the Russo-Turkish war with a circle of Turks lying flat on their faces (as if they were ashamed) round a newly-arrived shell.

There was a small hotel or shanty on the creek, on the main road, not far from the claim. Dave was desperate, and time flew much faster in his stimulated imagination than it did in reality, so he made for the shanty. There were several casual bushmen on the veranda and in the bar; Dave rushed into the bar, banging the door to behind him. 'My dog!' he gasped, in reply to the astonished stare of the publican, 'the blanky retriever – he's got a live cartridge in his mouth –'

The retriever, finding the front door shut against him, had bounded round and in by the back way, and now stood smiling in the doorway leading from the passage, the cartridge still in his mouth and the fuse spluttering. They burst out of that bar; Tommy bounded first after one and then after another, for, being a young dog, he tried to make friends with everybody.

The bushmen ran round corners, and some shut themselves in the stable. There was a new weatherboard and corrugated-iron kitchen and wash-house on piles in the backyard, with some women washing clothes inside. Dave and the publican bundled in there and shut the door – the publican cursing Dave and calling him a crimson fool, in hurried tones, and wanting to know what the hell he came here for.

The retriever went in under the kitchen, amongst the piles, but, luckily for those inside, there was a vicious yellow mongrel cattle-dog sulking and nursing his nastiness under there – a sneaking, fighting, thieving canine, whom neighbours had tried for years to shoot or poison. Tommy saw his danger – he'd had experience from this dog – and started out and across the yard, still sticking to the cartridge. Half-way across the yard the yellow dog caught him and nipped him. Tommy dropped the cartridge, gave one terrified yell, and took to the bush. The yellow dog followed him to the fence and then ran back to see what he had dropped. Nearly a dozen other dogs came from round all the corners and under the buildings – spidery, thievish, cold-blooded kangaroo-dogs, mongrel sheep- and cattle-dogs, vicious black and yellow dogs – that slip after you in the dark, nip your heels, and vanish without explaining – and yapping, yelping small fry. They kept at a respectable distance round the nasty yellow dog, for it was dangerous to go near him when he thought he had found something which might be good for a dog or cat. He sniffed at the cartridge twice, and was just taking a third cautious sniff when –

It was very good blasting-powder – a new brand that Dave had recently got up from Sydney; and the cartridge had been excellently well made. Andy was very patient and painstaking in all he did, and nearly as handy as the average sailor with needles, twine, canvas and rope.

Bushmen say that that kitchen jumped off its piles and on again. When the smoke and dust cleared away, the remains of the nasty yellow dog were lying against the paling fence of the yard looking as if it had been kicked into a fire by a horse and afterwards rolled in the dust under a barrow, and finally thrown against the fence from a distance. Several saddle-horses, which had been 'hanging-up' round the veranda, were galloping wildly down the road in clouds of dust, with broken bridle-reins flying; and from a circle round the outskirts, from every point of the compass in the scrub, came the yelping of dogs. Two of them went home, to the place where they were born, thirty miles away, and reached it the same night and stayed there; it was not till towards evening that the rest came back cautiously to make inquiries. One was trying to walk on two legs, and most of 'em looked more or less singed; and a little, singed, stumpy-tailed dog, who had been in the habit of hopping the back half of him along on one leg, had reason to be glad that he'd saved up the other leg all those years, for he needed it now. There was one old one-eyed cattle-dog round that shanty for years afterwards, who couldn't stand the smell of a gun being cleaned. He it was who had taken an interest, only second to that of the yellow dog, in the cartridge. Bushmen said that it was amusing to slip up on his blind side and stick a dirty ramrod under his nose: he wouldn't wait to bring his solitary eye to bear – he'd take to the bush and stay out all night.

For half an hour or so after the explosion there were several bushmen round behind the stable who crouched, doubled up, against the wall, or rolled gently on the dust, trying to laugh without shrieking. There were two white women in hysterics at the house, and a half-caste rushing aimlessly round with a dipper of cold water. The publican was holding his wife tight and begging her between her squawks, to 'Hold up for my sake, Mary, or I'll lam the life out of ye!'

Dave decided to apologize later on, 'when things had settled a bit', and went back to camp. And the dog that had done it all, Tommy, the great, idiotic mongrel retriever, came slobbering round Dave and lashing his legs with his tail, and trotted home after him, smiling his broadest, longest, and reddest smile of amiability, and apparently satisfied for one afternoon with the fun he'd had.

Andy chained the dog up securely, and cooked some more chops, while Dave went to help Jim out of the hole.

And most of this is why, for years afterwards, lanky, easy-going bushmen, riding lazily past Dave's camp, would cry, in a lazy drawl and with just a hint of the nasal twang:

''Ello, Da-a-ve! How's the fishin' getting on, Da-a-ve?'

To Build a Fire

JACK LONDON

Day had broken cold and grey, exceedingly cold and grey, when the man turned aside from the main Yukon trail and climbed the high earth-bank, where a dim and little-travelled trail led eastward through the fat spruce timberland. It was a steep bank, and he paused for breath at the top, excusing the act to himself by looking at his watch. It was nine o'clock. There was no sun nor hint of sun, though there was not a cloud in the sky. It was a clear day, and yet there seemed an intangible pall over the face of things, a subtle gloom that made the day dark, and that was due to the absence of sun. This fact did not worry the man. He was used to the lack of sun. It had been days since he had seen the sun, and he knew that a few more days must pass before that cheerful orb, due south, would just peep above the skyline and dip immediately from view.

The man flung a look back along the way he had come. The Yukon lay a mile wide and hidden under three feet of ice. On top of this ice were as many feet of snow. It was all pure white, rolling in gentle undulations where the ice jams of the freeze-up had formed. North and south, as far as his eye could see, it was unbroken white, save for a dark hairline that curved and twisted from around the spruce-covered island to the south and that curved and twisted away into the north, where it disappeared behind another spruce-covered island. This dark hairline was the trail – the main trail – that led south five hundred miles to the Chilcoot Pass, Dyea, and salt water; and that led north seventy miles to Dawson, and still on to the north a thousand miles to Nulato, and finally to St Michael, on Bering Sea, a thousand miles and half a thousand more.

But all this – the mysterious, far-reaching hairline trail, the absence of sun from the sky, the tremendous cold, and the strangeness and weirdness of it all – made no impression on the man. It was not because he was long used to it. He was a newcomer in the land, a *chechaquo*, and this was his first winter. The trouble with him was that he was without imagination. He was quick and alert in the things of life, but only in the things, and not in the significances. Fifty degrees below zero meant eighty-odd degrees of frost. Such fact impressed him as being cold and uncomfortable, and that was all. It did not lead him to meditate upon his frailty as a creature of temperature, and upon man's frailty in general, able only to live within certain narrow limits of heat and cold; and from there on it did not lead him to the conjectural field of immortality and man's place in the universe. Fifty degrees below zero stood for a bite of frost that hurt and that must be guarded against by the use of mittens, ear flaps, warm moccasins, and thick socks. Fifty degrees below zero. That there should be anything more to it than that was a thought that never entered his head.

As he turned to go on, he spat speculatively. There was a sharp explosive crackle that startled him. He spat again. And again, in the air, before it could fall to the snow, the spittle crackled. He knew that at fifty below spittle crackled on the snow, but this spittle had crackled in the air. Undoubtedly it was colder than fifty below – how much colder he did not know. But the temperature did not matter. He was bound for the old claim on the left fork of Henderson Creek, where the boys were already. They had come across the divide from the Indian Creek country, while he had come the roundabout way to take a look at the possibilities of getting out logs in the spring from the islands in the Yukon. He would be in to camp by six o'clock; a bit after dark, it was true, but the boys would be there, a fire would be going, and a hot supper would be ready. As for lunch, he pressed his hand against the protruding bundle under his jacket. It was also under his shirt, wrapped up in a handkerchief and lying against the naked skin. It was the only way to keep the biscuits from freezing. He smiled agreeably to himself as he thought of those biscuits, each cut open and sopped in bacon grease, and each enclosing a generous slice of fried bacon.

He plunged in among the big spruce trees. The trail was

faint. A foot of snow had falled since the last sled had passed over, and he was glad he was without a sled, travelling light. In fact, he carried nothing but the lunch wrapped in the handkerchief. He was surprised, however, at the cold. It certainly was cold, he concluded, as he rubbed his numb nose and cheekbones with his mittened hand. He was a warm-whiskered man, but the hair on his face did not protect the high cheekbones and the eager nose that thrust itself aggressively into the frosty air.

At the man's heels trotted a dog, a big native husky, the proper wolf-dog, grey-coated and without any visible or temperamental difference from its brother, the wild wolf. The animal was depressed by the tremendous cold. It knew that it was no time for travelling. Its instinct told it a truer tale than was told to the man by the man's judgment. In reality, it was not merely colder than fifty below zero; it was colder than sixty below, than seventy below. It was seventy-five below zero. Since the freezing point is thirty-two above zero, it meant that one hundred and seven degrees of frost obtained. The dog did not know anything about thermometers. Possibly in its brain there was no sharp consciousness of a condition of very cold such as was in the man's brain. But the brute had its instinct. It experienced a vague but menacing apprehension that subdued it and made it slink along at the man's heels, and that made it question eagerly every unwonted movement of the man as if expecting him to go into camp or to seek shelter somewhere and build a fire. The dog had learned fire, and it wanted fire, or else to burrow under the snow and cuddle its warmth away from the air.

The frozen moisture of its breathing had settled on its fur in a fine powder of frost, and especially were its jowls, muzzle, and eyelashes whitened by its crystal breath. The man's red beard and moustache were likewise frosted, but more solidly, the deposit taking the form of ice and increasing with every warm, moist breath he exhaled. Also, the man was chewing tobacco, and the muzzle of ice held his lips so rigidly that he was unable to clear his chin when he expelled the juice. The result was a crystal beard of the colour and solidity of amber

23

was increasing its length on his chin. If he fell down it would shatter itself, like glass, into brittle fragments. But he did not mind the appendage. It was the penalty all tobacco chewers paid in that country, and he had been out before in two cold snaps. They had not been so cold as this, he knew, but by the spirit thermometer at Sixty Mile he knew they had been registered at fifty below and at fifty-five.

He held on through the level stretch of woods for several miles, crossed a wide flat of nigger heads, and dropped down a bank to the frozen bed of a small stream. This was Henderson Creek, and he knew he was ten miles from the forks. He looked at his watch. It was ten o'clock. He was making four miles an hour, and he calculated that he would arrive at the forks at half-past twelve. He decided to celebrate that event by eating his lunch there.

The dog dropped in again at his heels, with a tail drooping discouragement, as the man swung along the creek bed. The furrow of the old sled trail was plainly visible, but a dozen inches of snow covered up the marks of the last runners. In a month no man had come up or down that silent creek. The man held steadily on. He was not much given to thinking, and just then particularly he had nothing to think about save that he would eat lunch at the forks and that at six o'clock he would be in camp with the boys. There was nobody to talk to; and, had there been, speech would have been impossible because of the ice muzzle on his mouth. So he continued monotonously to chew tobacco and to increase the length of his amber beard.

Once in a while the thought reiterated itself that it was very cold and that he had never experienced such cold. As he walked along he rubbed his cheekbones and nose with the back of his mittened hand. He did this automatically, now and again changing hands. But, rub as he would, the instant he stopped his cheekbones went numb, and the following instant the end of his nose went numb. He was sure to frost his cheeks; he knew that, and experienced a pang of regret that he had not devised a nose strap of the sort Bud wore in cold snaps. Such a strap passed across the cheeks, as well, and saved them. But it didn't matter much, after all. What were

24

frosted cheeks? A bit painful, that was all; they were never serious.

Empty as the man's mind was of thoughts, he was keenly observant, and he noticed the changes in the creeks, the curves and bends and timber jams, and always he sharply noted where he placed his feet. Once, coming round a bend, he shied abruptly, like a startled horse, curved away from the place where he had been walking, and retreated several paces back along the trail. The creek he knew was frozen clear to the bottom – no creek could contain water in that Arctic winter – but he knew also that there were springs that bubbled out from the hillsides and ran along under the snow and on top of the ice of the creek. He knew that the coldest snaps never froze these springs, and he knew likewise their danger. They were traps. They hid pools of water under the snow that might be three inches deep, or three feet. Sometimes a skin of ice half an inch thick covered them, and in turn was covered by the snow. Sometimes there were alternate layers of water and ice skin, so that when one broke through he kept on breaking through for a while, sometimes wetting himself to the waist.

That was why he had shied in such a panic. He had felt the give under his feet and heard the crackle of a snow-hidden ice skin. And to get his feet wet in such a temperature meant trouble and danger. At the very least it meant delay, for he would be forced to stop and build a fire, and under its protection to bare his feet while he dried his socks and moccasins. He stood and studied the creek bed and its banks, and decided that the flow of water came from the right. He reflected awhile, rubbing his nose and cheeks, then skirted to the left, stepping gingerly and testing the footing for each step. Once clear of the danger, he took a fresh chew of tobacco and swung along at his four-mile gait.

In the course of the next two hours he came upon several similar traps. Usually the snow above the hidden pools had a sunken, candied appearance that advertised the danger. Once again, however, he had a close call; and once, suspecting danger, he compelled the dog to go on in front. The dog did not want to go. It hung back until the man shoved it forward,

25

and then it went quickly across the white, unbroken surface. Suddenly it broke through, floundered to one side, and got away to firmer footing. It had wet its forefeet and legs, and almost immediately the water that clung to it turned to ice. It made quick efforts to lick the ice off its legs, then dropped down in the snow and began to bite out the ice that had formed between the toes. This was a matter of instinct. To permit the ice to remain would mean sore feet. It did not know this. It merely obeyed the mysterious prompting that arose from the deep crypts of its being. But the man knew, having achieved a judgment on the subject, and he removed the mitten from his right hand and helped to tear out the ice particles. He did not expose his fingers more than a minute, and was astonished at the swift numbness that smote them. It certainly was cold. He pulled on the mitten hastily, and beat the hand savagely across his chest.

At twelve o'clock the day was at its brightest. Yet the sun was too far south on its winter journey to clear the horizon. The bulge of the earth intervened between it and Henderson Creek, where the man walked under a clear sky at noon and cast no shadow. At half-past twelve, to the minute, he arrived at the forks of the creek. He was pleased at the speed he had made. If he kept it up, he would certainly be with the boys by six. He unbuttoned his jacket and shirt and drew forth his lunch. The action consumed no more than a quarter of a minute, yet in that brief moment the numbness laid hold of the exposed fingers. He did not put the mitten on, but, instead, struck the fingers a dozen sharp smashes against his leg. Then he sat down on a snow-covered log to eat. The sting that followed upon the striking of his fingers against his leg ceased so quickly that he was startled. He had had no chance to take a bite of biscuit. He struck the fingers repeatedly and returned them to the mitten, baring the other hand for the purpose of eating. He tried to take a mouthful, but the ice muzzle prevented. He had forgotten to build a fire and thaw out. He chuckled at his foolishness, and as he chuckled he noted the numbness creeping into the exposed fingers. Also, he noted that the stinging which had first come to his toes when he sat down was already passing away. He wondered whether the toes were warm or numb. He moved them inside the moccasins and decided that they were numb.

He pulled the mitten on hurriedly and stood up. He was a bit frightened. He stamped up and down until the stinging returned into the feet. It certainly was cold, was his thought. That man from Sulphur Creek had spoken the truth when telling how cold it sometimes got in the country. And he had laughed at him at the time! That showed one must not be too sure of things. There was no mistake about it, it *was* cold. He strode up and down, stamping his feet and threshing his arms, until reassured by the returning warmth. Then he got out matches and proceeded to make a fire. From the undergrowth, where high water of the previous spring had lodged a supply of seasoned twigs, he got his firewood. Working carefully from a small beginning, he soon had a roaring fire, over which he thawed the ice from his face and in the protection of which he ate his biscuits. For the moment the cold of space was outwitted. The dog took satisfaction in the fire, stretching out close enough for warmth and far enough away to escape being singed.

When the man had finished, he filled his pipe and took his comfortable time over a smoke. Then he pulled on his mittens, settled the ear-flaps of his cap firmly about his ears, and took the creek trail up the left fork. The dog was disappointed and yearned back towards the fire. This man did not know cold. Possibly all the generations of his ancestry had been ignorant of cold, of real cold, of cold one hundred and seven degrees below freezing point. But the dog knew; all its ancestry knew, and it had inherited the knowledge. And it knew that it was not good to walk abroad in such fearful cold. It was the time to lie snug in a hole in the snow and wait for a curtain of cloud to be drawn across the face of outer space whence this cold came. On the other hand, there was no keen intimacy between the dog and the man. The one was the toil slave of the other, and the only caresses it had ever received were the caresses of the whip lash and of harsh and menacing throat sounds that threatened the whip lash. So the dog made no effort to communicate its apprehension to the man. It was not concerned in the welfare of the man; it was for its own sake that it yearned back towards the fire. But the man whistled, and spoke to it with the sound of whip lashes, and the dog swung in at the man's heels and followed after.

The man took a chew of tobacco and proceeded to start a new amber beard. Also, his moist breath quickly powdered with white his moustache, eyebrows, and lashes. There did not seem to be so many springs on the left fork of the Henderson, and for half an hour the man saw no signs of any. And then it happened. At a place where there were no signs, where the soft, unbroken snow seemed to advertise solidity beneath, the man broke through. It was not deep. He wet himself half-way to the knees before he floundered out to the firm crust.

He was angry, and cursed his luck aloud. He had hoped to get into camp with the boys at six o'clock, and this would delay him an hour, for he would have to build a fire and dry out his footgear. This was imperative at that low temperature – he knew that much; and he turned aside to the bank, which he climbed. On top, tangled in the underbrush about the trunks of several small spruce trees, was a high-water deposit of dry firewood – sticks and twigs, principally, but also larger portions of seasoned branches and fine, dry, last year's grasses. He threw down several large pieces on top of the snow. This served for a foundation and prevented the young flame from drowning itself in the snow it otherwise would melt. The flame he got by touching a match to a small shred of birch bark that he took from his pocket. This burned even more readily than paper. Placing it on the foundation, he fed the young flame with wisps of dry grass and with the tiniest dry twigs.

He worked slowly and carefully, keenly aware of his danger. Gradually, as the flame grew stronger, he increased the size of the twigs with which he fed it. He squatted in the snow pulling the twigs out from their entanglement in the brush and feeding directly to the flame. He knew there must be no failure. When it is seventy-five below zero, a man must not fail in his first attempt to build a fire – that is, if his feet are wet. If his feet are dry, and he fails, he can run along the trail for half a mile and

28

restore his circulation. But the circulation of wet and freezing feet cannot be restored by running when it is seventy-five below. No matter how fast he runs, the wet feet will freeze the harder.

All this the man knew. The old-timer on Sulphur Creek had told him about it the previous fall, and now he was appreciating the advice. Already all sensation had gone out of his feet. To build the fire he had been forced to remove his mittens, and the fingers had quickly gone numb. His pace of four miles an hour had kept his heart pumping blood to the surface of his body and to all the extremities. But the instant he stopped, the action of the pump eased down. The cold of space smote the unprotected tip of the planet, and he, being on that unprotected tip, received the full force of the blow. The blood of his body recoiled before it. The blood was alive, like the dog, and like the dog it wanted to hide away and cover itself up from the fearful cold. So long as he walked four miles an hour, he pumped that blood willy-nilly, to the surface; but now it ebbed away and sank down into the recesses of his body. The extremities were the first to feel its absence. His wet feet froze the faster, and his exposed fingers numbed the faster, though they had not yet begun to freeze. Nose and cheeks were already freezing, while the skin of all his body chilled as it lost its blood.

But he was safe. Toes and nose and cheeks would be only touched by the frost, for the fire was beginning to burn with strength. He was feeding it with twigs the size of his finger. In another minute he would be able to feed it with branches the size of his wrist, and then he could remove his wet footgear, and, while it dried, he could keep his naked feet warm by the fire, rubbing them at first, of course with snow. The fire was a success. He was safe. He remembered the advice of the old-timer on Sulphur Creek, and smiled. The old-timer had been very serious in laying down the law that no man must travel alone in the Klondike after fifty below. Well, here he was; he had had the accident; he was alone; and he had saved himself. Those old-timers were rather womanish, some of them, he thought. All a man had to do was to keep his head, and he was all right. Any man who was a man could travel alone. But it was surprising, the rapidity with which his cheeks and nose were freezing. And he had not thought his fingers could go lifeless in so short a time. Lifeless they were, for he could scarcely make them move together to grip a twig, and they seemed remote from his body and from him. When he touched a twig, he had to look and see whether or not he had hold of it. The wires were pretty well down between him and his finger ends.

All of which counted for little. There was the fire, snapping and crackling and promising life with every dancing flame. He started to untie his moccasins. They were coated with ice; the thick German socks were like sheaths of iron halfway to the knees; and the moccasin strings were like rods of steel all twisted and knotted as by some conflagration. For a moment he tugged with his numb fingers, then, realizing the folly of it, he drew his sheath knife.

But before he could cut the strings, it happened. It was his own fault or, rather, his mistake. He should not have built the fire under the spruce tree. He should have built it in the open. But it had been easier to pull the twigs from the brush and drop them directly on the fire. Now the tree under which he had done this carried a weight of snow on its boughs. No wind had blown for weeks, and each bough was fully freighted. Each time he had pulled a twig he had communicated a slight agitation to the tree – an imperceptible agitation, so far as he was concerned, but an agitation sufficient to bring about the disaster. High up in the tree one bough capsized its load of snow. This fell on the boughs beneath, capsizing them. This process continued, spreading out and involving the whole tree. It grew like an avalanche, and it descended without warning upon the man and the fire, and the fire was blotted out! Where it had burned was a mantle of fresh and disordered snow.

The man was shocked. It was as though he had just heard his own sentence of death. For a moment he sat and stared at the spot where the fire had been. Then he grew very calm. Perhaps the old-timer on Sulphur Creek was right. If he had only had a trail mate he would have been in no danger now.

The trail mate could have built the fire. Well, it was up to him to build the fire over again, and this second time there must be no failure. Even if he succeeded, he would most likely lose some toes. His feet must be badly frozen by now, and there would be some time before the second fire was ready.

Such were his thoughts, but he did not sit and think them. He was busy all the time they were passing through his mind. He made a new foundation for a fire, this time in the open, where no treacherous tree could blot it out. Next he gathered dry grasses and tiny twigs from the high-water flotsam. He could not bring his fingers together to pull them out, but he was able to gather them by the handful. In this way he got many rotten twigs and bits of green moss that were undesirable, but it was the best he could do. He worked methodically, even collecting an armful of the larger branches to be used later when the fire gathered strength. And all the while the dog sat and watched him, a certain yearning wistfulness in its eyes, for it looked upon him as the fire provider, and the fire was slow in coming.

When all was ready, the man reached in his pocket for a second piece of birch bark. He knew the bark was there, and, though he could not feel it with his fingers, he could hear its crisp rustling as he fumbled for it. Try as he would, he could not clutch hold of it. And all the time, in his consciousness, was the knowledge that each instant his feet were freezing. This thought tended to put him in a panic, but he fought against it and kept calm. He pulled on his mittens with his teeth, and threshed his arms back and forth, beating his hands with all his might against his sides. He did this sitting down, and he stood up to do it; and all the while the dog sat in the snow, its wolf brush of a tail curled around warmly over its forefront, its sharp wolf ears pricked forward intently as it watched the man. And the man, as he beat and threshed with his arms and hands, felt a great surge of envy as he regarded the creature that was warm and secure in its natural covering.

After a time he was aware of the first faraway signals of sensation in his beaten fingers. The faint tingling grew stronger till it evolved into a stinging ache that was excruciating, but which the man hailed with satisfaction. He stripped the mitten from his right hand and fetched forth the birch bark. The exposed fingers were quickly going numb again. Next he brought out his bunch of sulphur matches. But the tremendous cold had already driven the life out of his fingers. In his effort to separate one match from the others, the whole bunch fell in the snow. He tried to pick it out of the snow, but failed. The dead fingers could neither touch nor clutch. He was very careful. He drove the thought of his freezing feet, and nose, and cheeks, out of his mind, devoting his whole soul to the matches. He watched, using the sense of vision in place of that of touch, and when he saw his fingers on each side the bunch, he closed them – that is, he willed to close them, for the wires were down, and the fingers did not obey. He pulled the mitten on the right hand, and beat it fiercely against his knee. Then with both mittened hands, he scooped the bunch of matches, along with much snow, into his lap. Yet he was no better off.

After some manipulation he managed to get the bunch between the heels of his mittened hands. In this fashion he carried it to his mouth. The ice crackled and snapped when by a violent effort he opened his mouth. He drew the lower jaw in, curled the upper lip out of the way, and scraped the bunch with his upper teeth in order to separate a match. He succeeded in getting one, which he dropped on his lap. He was no better off. He could not pick it up. Then he devised a way. He picked it up in his teeth and scratched it on his leg. Twenty times he scratched before he succeeded in lighting it. As it flamed he held it with his teeth to the birch bark. But the burning brimstone went up his nostrils and into his lungs, causing him to cough spasmodically. The match fell into the snow and went out.

The old-timer on Sulphur Creek was right, he thought in the moment of controlled despair that ensued: after fifty below, a man should travel with a partner. He beat his hands, but failed in exciting any sensation. Suddenly he bared both hands, removing the mittens with his teeth. He caught the whole bunch between the heels of his hands. His arm muscles not being frozen enabled him to press the hand heels tightly against

32

the matches. Then he scratched the bunch along his leg. It flared into flame, seventy sulphur matches at once! There was no wind to blow them out. He kept his head to one side to escape the strangling fumes, and held the blazing bunch to the birch bark. As he so held it, he become aware of sensation in his hand. His flesh was burning. He could smell it. Deep down below the surface he could feel it. The sensation developed into pain that grew acute. And still he endured it, holding the flame of the matches clumsily to the bark that would not light readily because his own burning hands were in the way, absorbing most of the flame.

At last, when he could endure no more, he jerked his hands apart. The blazing matches fell sizzling into the snow, but the birch bark was alight. He began laying dry grasses and the tiniest twigs on the flame. He could not pick and choose, for he had to lift the fuel between the heels of his hands. Small pieces of rotten wood and green moss clung to the twigs, and he bit them off as well as he could with his teeth. He cherished the flame carefully and awkwardly. It meant life, and it must not perish. The withdrawal of blood from the surface of his body now made him begin to shiver, and he grew more awkward. A large piece of green moss fell squarely on the little fire. He tried to poke it out with his fingers, but his shivering frame made him poke too far, and he disrupted the nucleus of the little fire, the burning grasses and tiny twigs separating and scattering. He tried to poke them together again, but in spite of the tenseness of the effort, his shivering got away with him, and the twigs were hopelessly scattered. Each twig gushed a puff of smoke and went out. The fire provider had failed. As he looked apathetically about him, his eyes chanced on the dog, sitting across the ruins of the fire from him, in the snow, making restless, hunching movements, slightly lifting one forefoot and then the other, shifting its weight back and forth on them with wistful eagerness.

The sight of the dog put a wild idea into his head. He remembered the tale of the man, caught in a blizzard, who killed a steer and crawled inside the carcase, and so was saved. He would kill the dog and bury his hands in the warm body

33

until the numbness went out of them. Then he could build another fire. He spoke to the dog, calling it to him; but in his voice was a strange note of fear that frightened the animal, who had never known the man to speak in such a way before. Something was the matter, and its suspicious nature sensed danger – it knew not what danger, but somewhere, somehow, in its brain arose an apprehension of the man. It flattened its ears down at the sound of the man's voice, and its restless, hunching movements and the liftings and shiftings of its forefeet became more pronounced; but it would not come to the man. He got on his hands and knees and crawled towards the dog. This unusual posture again excited suspicion, and the animal sidled mincingly away.

The man sat up in the snow for a moment and struggled for calmness. Then he pulled on his mittens, by means of his teeth, and got upon his feet. He glanced down at first in order to assure himself that he was really standing up, for the absence of sensation in his feet left him unrelated to the earth. His erect position in itself started to drive the webs of suspicion from the dog's mind; and when he spoke peremptorily, with the sound of whip lashes in his voice, the dog rendered its customary allegiance and came to him. As it came within reaching distance, the man lost his control. His arms flashed out to the dog, and he experienced genuine surprise when he discovered that his hands could not clutch, that there was neither bend nor feeling in the fingers. He had forgotten for the moment that they were frozen and that they were freezing more and more. All this happened quickly, and before the animal could get away, he encircled its body with his arms. He sat down in the snow, and in this fashion held the dog, while it snarled and whined and struggled.

But it was all he could do, hold its body encircled in his arms and sit there. He realized he could not kill the dog. There was no way to do it. With his helpless hands he could neither draw nor hold his sheath knife nor throttle the animal. He released it, and it plunged wildly away, with tail between its legs, and still snarling. It halted forty feet away and surveyed him curiously, with ears sharply pricked forward.

34

The man looked down at his hands in order to locate them, and found them hanging on the ends of his arms. It struck him as curious that one should have to use his eyes in order to find out where his hands were. He began threshing his arms back and forth, beating the mittened hands against his sides. He did this for five minutes, violently, and his heart pumped enough blood up to the surface to put a stop to his shivering. But no sensation was aroused in the hands. He had an impression that they hung like weights on the ends of his arms, but when he tried to run the impression down, he could not find it.

A certain fear of death, dull and oppressive, came to him. This fear quickly became poignant as he realized that it was no longer a mere matter of freezing his fingers and toes, or of losing his hands and feet, but that it was a matter of life and death with the chances against him. This threw him into a panic, and he turned and ran up the creek bed along the old, dim trail. The dog joined in behind him and kept up with him. He ran blindly, without intention, in fear such as he had never known in his life. Slowly, as he ploughed and floundered through the snow, he began to see things again – the banks of the creek, the old timber jams, the leafless aspens, and the sky. The running made him feel better. He did not shiver. Maybe, if he ran on, his feet would thaw out; and, anyway, if he ran far enough, he would reach camp and the boys. Without doubt he would lose some fingers and toes and some of his face; but the boys would take care of him, and save the rest of him when he got there. And at the same time there was another thought in his mind that said he would never get to the camp and the boys; that it was too many miles away, that the freezing had too great a start on him, and that he would soon be stiff and dead. This thought he kept in the background and refused to consider. Sometimes it pushed itself forward and demanded to be heard, but he thrust it back and strove to think of other things.

It struck him as curious that he could run at all on feet so frozen that he could not feel them when they struck the earth and took the weight of his body. He seemed to himself to skim along the surface, and to have no connection with the earth. Somewhere he had once seen a winged Mercury, and he wondered if Mercury felt as he felt when skimming over the earth.

His theory of running until he reached camp and the boys had one flaw in it: he lacked the endurance. Several times he stumbled, and finally he tottered, crumpled up, and fell. When he tried to rise, he failed. He must sit and rest, he decided, and next time he would merely walk and keep on going. As he sat and regained his breath, he noted that he was feeling quite warm and comfortable. He was not shivering, and it even seemed that a warm glow had come to his chest and trunk. And yet, when he touched his nose or cheeks, there was no sensation. Running would not thaw them out. Nor would it thaw out his hands and feet. Then the thought came to him that the frozen portions of his body must be extending. He tried to keep this thought down, to forget it, to think of something else; he was aware of the panicky feeling that it caused, and he was afraid of the panic. But the thought asserted itself, and persisted, until it produced a vision of his body totally frozen. This was too much, and he made another wild run along the trail. Once he slowed down to a walk, but the thought of the freezing extending itself made him run again.

And all the time the dog ran with him, at his heels. When he fell down a second time, it curled its tail over its forefeet and sat in front of him, facing him, curiously eager and intent. The warmth and security of the animal angered him, and he cursed it till it flattened down its ears appeasingly. This time the shivering came more quickly upon the man. He was losing in his battle with the frost. It was creeping into his body from all sides. The thought of it drove him on, but he ran no more than a hundred feet, when he staggered and pitched headlong. It was his last panic. When he had recovered his breath and control, he sat up and entertained in his mind the conception of meeting death with dignity. However, the conception did not come to him in such terms. His idea of it was that he had been making a fool of himself, running around like a chicken with its head cut off – such was the simile that occurred to him. Well, he was bound to freeze anyway, and he might as well take it decently. With this new-found peace of mind came the first glimmerings of drowsiness. A good idea, he thought, to sleep off to death. It was like taking an anaesthetic. Freezing was not so bad as people thought. There were lots worse ways to die.

He pictured the boys finding his body next day. Suddenly he found himself with them, coming along the trail looking for himself. And, still with them, he came around a turn in the trail and found himself lying in the snow. He did not belong with himself any more, for even then he was out of himself, standing with the boys and looking at himself in the snow. It certainly was cold, was his thought. When he got back to the States he could tell the folks what real cold was. He drifted on from this to a vision of the old-timer on Sulphur Creek. He could see him quite clearly, warm and comfortable, and smoking a pipe.

'You were right, old hoss; you were right,' the man mumbled to the old-timer of Sulphur Creek.

Then the man drowsed off into what seemed to him the most comfortable and satisfying sleep he had ever known. The dog sat facing him and waiting. The brief day drew to a close in a long, slow twilight. There were no signs of a fire to be made, and, besides, never in the dog's experience had it known a man to sit like that in the snow and make no fire. As the twilight drew on, its eager yearning for the fire mastered it, and with a great lifting and shifting of forefeet, it whined softly, then flattened its ears down in anticipation of being chidden by the man. But the man remained silent. Later the dog whined loudly. And still later it crept close to the man and caught the scent of death. This made the animal bristle and back away. A little longer it delayed, howling under the stars that leaped and danced and shone brightly in the cold sky. Then it turned and trotted up the trail in the direction of the camp it knew, where were the other food providers and fire providers.

Vaarlem and Tripp

LEON GARFIELD

It's certain he has a great gift: but otherwise he is a very contemptible, vile little man – strong-smelling, even, and well known in the Amsterdam courts for fraud, embezzlement and bankruptcy. It's very humiliating to be his pupil, but, as my father says, if God has planted a lily in a cess-pit, one must stop up one's nose and go down. Of late, my task has been to choose his brushes, pigment and canvas. He tells me this is as important a part of the craft of painting as there is, but the truth of the matter is that he's so much in debt and disgrace that he daren't show his face outside the studio. My name is Roger Vaarlem; my master is Joseph Tripp, of course.

A month ago he was before the Burghers who told him his portrait of the Admiral was unacceptable – insulting, even – and demanded their advance of guilders back. Having spent it, he offered to paint the Admiral again, but was not trusted: and rightly. Truth to Nature was one thing (no one could deny the portrait had a deal of truth in it, for my master has his gift), but truth to one's country and employers must come first. So he was given the opportunity of redeeming himself by painting a grand battle-piece to be hung in the Town Hall. Or prosecution in the courts again. Angrily (he told me) he accepted, and was granted a cabin aboard the *Little Willelm*. We sailed at half past eight this morning.

Though the early morning had been warm and brilliant, he was muffled in every garment he could find, careless of their cleanliness, which is a strong point aboard Dutch ships. It was very shameful to be walking along beside him, carrying his sketchbooks and other belongings which smelled worse than the tar and pickled fish with which the air was strong. There were two ships of ninety guns nodding in a stately fashion

38

upon the gentle tide: cathedrals of gilded wood with triple spires and delicate crosses, netted and festooned like for a Saint's Day. The thought crossed my mind of parting from Mynheer Tripp and going to sea on my own, but my father would have prosecuted him for negligence and fraud and he'd have gone to gaol for it.

Then we came to the *Little Willelm* and he at once began to complain that it was insufficiently armed and pointed out the maze of stitching on the fore-topsail where English musket-fire had peppered it to a sieve. Together with all his other qualities, he is a great coward and I felt myself blush as he ranted on in the hearing of one of the ship's officers. Then, with my hand to his elbow, he went aboard, stepping down on the deck as if it were a single floating plank and not secure.

The *Little Willelm*, being but a smallish barquentine, could offer only a tiny cabin next to the surgeon's; but at least it was clean which flattered Mynheer Tripp unwarrantably.

'Go away, Vaarlem!' he mumbled, and crawled on to the bunk – for the motion of the ship at its moorings was already unsettling his stomach. So I left him and went out on to the maindeck in the sunny air and watched the crew go about their business in the rigging and on the yards.

'How come a fine-looking lad like you goes about with an old rag-bag like him?'

Mynheer Leyden – an officer of good family – was standing by me.

I answered: 'Sir – he's a great man, whatever you may think, and will be remembered long after you and me are forgot.'

After all, one has one's pride!

Mynheer Leyden would have answered, but Captain Kuyper began shouting from the quarter-deck to cast off and Mynheer Leyden shrugged his smooth shoulders and went about his duties. These seemed to consist in putting his hands behind his back and pacing the larboard rail, nodding to the crowd of fishwives and early clerks who always throng the harbour in the mornings to watch the glorious ships heave and puff out their sails like proud white chests and lean their way into the dangerous sea.

Once out of the harbour, the foresail was set and I went below to inform Mynheer Tripp he was missing a very wonderful sight, for there was not much wind and the great spread of canvas seemed to be but breathing against invisible, creaking stays. But he was already up and about – and in a more cheerful mood. He'd had intelligence that the *Little Willelm* was to sail west by south-west to lure enemy vessels into pursuit, when they'd be blown out of the water by our own great ships which would be following on the next tide. His cheerfulness arose from the discovery that the *Little Willelm* was the swiftest vessel in the Channel and was not intended to fight.

'A clean pair of heels, eh? Ha-ha!' he kept saying . . . and grinning in a very unwholesome manner. It was the only time I'd ever known him take a real pleasure in cleanliness. Later on, his spirits rose high enough for him to behave in his usual way. He began soliciting guilders from the officers to portray them prominently in the battle-piece. Full of shame – for he was earning a good deal of contempt – I warned him he'd be prosecuted for false pretences.

'Why?' he muttered angrily – the wind catching the soft brim of his black hat and smacking his face with it.

'Because they won't be larger than thumb-nails, sir!'

'You mind your own business, Vaarlem!' he snarled, quite beside himself where guilders were concerned. 'If those little tinsel nobodies tell their dough-faced relatives that such and such a blob of paint is their darling – well? Why not? What's wrong with a little family pride? Immortal, that's what they'll be! So keep your middle-class nose out of my affairs, Master Vaarlem . . . or I'll paint you as an Englishman!'

He stalked away, holding his hat with one hand and his filthy shawls and oil-stained coat with the other. But soon after, he sidled back again and remarked ingratiatingly, 'No need to tell your papa everything I say, Roger, dear lad . . . words spoke in haste . . . no need for misunderstandings, eh? Dear boy . . .'

He was so mean, he was frightened my father would withdraw me as his pupil – and with me would go guilders. I looked at him coldly, while he bit his lip and brooded uneasily on whether he'd cut off his nose to spite his face; not that either would have been the loser.

I was more offended than I cared to let him know, so I obliged by keeping my nose out of his affairs for the remainder of the day. Which wasn't difficult, as he kept to the great cabin with the surgeon. Not that he was really ill – God forbid! – but he was cunningly picking the surgeon's wits relative to every ache and pain that plagued him. While all the while, the simple surgeon was happily imagining himself in the forefront of the Town Hall's battle-piece, a hero for ever. (Mynheer Tripp did indeed make a small sketch of him: a very wonderful piece of work – for somehow he caught a look of bewilderment and embarrassment in the surgeon's eyes as if God had too often stared them out.)

I'd intended to leave him for much longer than I did; at one time in the day I'd very serious thoughts indeed of leaving him altogether and fighting for Holland. This was when we saw our first English sail and there was great activity on the lower gun-deck against the chance of an encounter. She was a handsome, warlike vessel, bosoming strongly along. 'A seventy-four,' remarked Mynheer Leyden briskly. 'By tomorrow she'll be drift-wood!' Then we outpaced her and the sea was as clean as a German silver tray.

It was a few minutes before half past eight o'clock in the evening. I'd been on deck together with several officers. The wind was gone. The air was still. A sharp-edged quarter moon seemed to have sliced the clouds into strips, so that they fell away slowly, leaving dark threads behind. Earlier, Mynheer Leyden had been urging me to speak with the captain relative to my becoming a midshipman, for I was of good family and too good for Mynheer Tripp. To be a painter was a lower-class ambition. ('All right! He has his gift! But what's that to you and me? God gave him sharp eyes – but He gave us good families! Vaarlem, my boy – I can't make you out!') Then, a few minutes before half past eight, he said quietly, 'Vaarlem: you'd best go down and fetch him.' Which I did.

'Sir: you must come up on deck at once.'

Mynheer Tripp glanced at me irritably, began to mumble something, then thought better of it. He stood up and wrapped himself in the filthy shawls and coat he'd strewn about the cabin.

'Hurry, sir!'

'Why? The sea won't run away . . . and if it does, I shan't be sorry!' He followed me on to the deck.

'Look, Mynheer Tripp! The Englishman!'

For a proud moment, I thought he'd had enough brandy to make him behave like a Dutchman, for he stood quite still and silent. Then the brandy's effect wore off and his own miserable spirit shone through. Every scrap of colour went from his face and he began to tremble with terror and rage!

'Madmen!' he shrieked – and I wished myself at the bottom of the sea and Mynheer Tripp with me. The Englishman was within half a kilometre, and still moving softly towards us, pulled by two longboats whose oars pricked little silver buds in the moonswept sea. She was as silent as the grave, and any moment now would turn, broadside on, and greet us with the roar of thirty-seven iron mouths. For she was the seventy-four.

Mynheer Tripp seized my arm and began dragging me towards the quarter-deck, shouting outrageously: 'Move off! For God's sake move off! We'll all be killed! How dare you do such a thing! Look! Look! This boy . . . of a good family . . . very important! If he's harmed I'll be prosecuted by his father. And so will you! I demand to go back! For Vaarlem's sake! Oh, my God! A battle!'

They must have heard him aboard the Englishman. I could only pray that no one aboard it knew Dutch! I felt myself go as red as a poppy. To be used by this villainous coward as a mean excuse – I all but fought with him!

'You pig, Mynheer Tripp!' I panted. 'This time you've gone too far!'

'Pig?' he hissed, between roarings at the captain. 'You shut your middle-class mouth, Master Vaarlem! These noodles have no right to expose me – us to such danger! I'll sue – that's what I'll do! In the courts!'

Captain Kuyper – a man who'd faced death a hundred times

42

and now faced it for maybe the last – stared at Mynheer Tripp as if from a great distance.

'You are perfectly right, sir. This ship is no place for you. You will be put off in the boat and rowed to where you may observe the engagement in safety. Or go to Holland. Or go to Hell, sir! As for the boy – he may stay if he chooses. I would not be ashamed to die in *his* company.'

To my astonishment, before I could answer – and God knows what I'd have said – Mynheer Tripp burst out with: 'How dare you, sir, put such ideas into a boy's head! What d'you expect him to say? A boy of good family like him! Unfair, sir! Cruel! Dishonest! What can he know? I warn you, if you don't put him off, I'll not stir from your miserable ship! Both of us – or none! Oh, there'll be trouble! In the courts!'

Then he turned his mean, inflamed face towards me and muttered urgently: 'Keep quiet, Vaarlem! None of your business! Don't you dare say a word! I forbid it!'

Captain Kuyper shrugged his shoulders and turned away. 'Put them both in the boat, and let one man go with them to take the oars. Immediately! I want Mynheer Tripp off this ship at once. Or by God, I'll throw him off!'

Quite sick with shame, I followed Mynheer Tripp, who'd scuttled to the boat and hopped into it, clutching his sketch-books and horrible clothes about him – in a panic that the captain would do him a mischief.

The sailor who rowed us was a tall, silent fellow by the name of Krebs. For about twenty minutes he said nothing but rowed with a seemingly slow, but steady stroke. Mynheer Tripp, his head hunched into his shoulders, grasped my wrist and stared at the diminishing bulk of the *Little Willelm* which lay between us and the huge Englishman. Implacably, the Englishman came nearer and nearer and still did not turn. We could no more see the longboats . . . but the men in them must have had nerves of iron, for they were within musket range of the *Little Willelm* and could have been shot to pieces.

'Faster! Faster!' urged my master, as the bowsprit of the Englishman appeared to nod above the *Willelm*'s deck. There looked to be no more than fifty metres between them. Then she began to slew round . . . ponderously . . . malignantly. . . .

'Will you watch from here, sirs?' Krebs had stopped rowing. There was nothing contemptuous in the way he spoke. He simply wanted to know.

'Is it – is it safe?'

Krebs eyed the distance. 'Most likely – yes, sir.'

The two ships now lay side by side – the Englishman's aft projecting beyond the *Willelm*. Her after-castle, much gilded and gleaming under three lanterns, rose nearly as high as the *Willelm*'s mizen yard. A very unequal encounter. Perhaps she thought so? And was waiting for a surrender?

Krebs shipped his oars and stuck his chin in his great hands. Calmly he stared at the dark shape of his own ship, outlined against the sombre, spiky brown of her enemy. Though the shrouds and yards must have been alive with marksmen, nothing stirred to betray them.

'Thank God we ain't aboard!' he remarked at length. Mynheer Tripp nodded vigorously. He'd begun to make sketches by the light of a small lantern. Approvingly, Krebs glanced at them. Very workmanlike. I began to feel cold and lonely. Was I the only one who wished himself back aboard the *Little Willelm*?

The beginnings of a breeze. The great ghostly sails of the Englishman began to shift, but not quite to fill. The *Willelm*'s sails being smaller, bellied out more fatly. The bold little Dutchman and the skinny Englishman began to move. Masts, which had seemed all of one ship, began to divide – to part asunder. . . .

There seemed to be a moment of extraordinary stillness – even breathlessness – when suddenly a huge yellow flower of fire grew out of the side of the Englishman. (Beautiful Dutch lady – take my murdering bouquet!)

And then enormous billows of reddish smoke roared and blossomed up, blundering through the rigging and fouling the sails and sky. The engagement was begun.

A faint sound of screaming and shouting reached us, but was instantly drowned in the roar of the *Willelm*'s broadside. Then the Englishman fired again – this time with grapeshot, which makes an amazing, shrieking sound as it flies.

44

'The mainmast! D'you see? They've got the mainmast!' muttered Krebs, his face white even in the reddish glare of the encounter. 'Shrouds and halyards cut through – murder for them on deck! Slices them in two and three parts! Murder, it is!'

The *Willelm* was still firing – but not full broadsides. Half her ports must have been shattered.

'They've got to heave the dead out of the way!' Krebs said very urgently – as if it was his immediate task. 'Can't get to the powder quick enough with all them dead tangling up the trunnions . . . got to heave 'em out . . . Cap'n'll be down there now – he'll be doing the right thing –'

Another flash and roar from the Englishman : not so vast as the first. Was she disabled, too?

'Quarter-deck cannon,' mumbled Krebs, suddenly scowling. 'Now you'll see –' Again, she roared. 'Upper deck cannon . . . fourteen killers there!' A third blaze and roar. Krebs nodded. 'Lower deck. They know what they're at. Give no chance . . . no chance at all. . . .'

The *Willelm* seemed to have stopped firing. 'Look! Poor devils up in the cross-trees. D'ye see? Firebrands! Nought else left! But they'll never reach to the Englishman. Poor devils! Oh, God! She's afire herself! Keep your heads down, sirs! She'll be going up in a minute! A-ah!'

Even as he spoke, the fire must have reached the *Willelm*'s powder store. There was a glare and a thunderous crackling sound like the end of the world – as indeed for many it was. With a shriek of terror, Mynheer Tripp – who'd been extraordinarily absorbed throughout the encounter, oblivious to everything but his rapid, intent drawing – flung himself to the bottom of the boat: a quaking bundle of disgusting rags. Then the great light went out of the sky and the air was full of smoke and the sharp, bitter smell of spent powder and burnt out lives. Pieces of wood began to kiss the water about us. When at last the smoke drifted up to the moon, we saw the guilty hump of the Englishman sliding away, leaving nothing more behind than a torn-up patch of sea, rough with driftwood and darknesses.

'Oh, God! Now what's to become of us?' wept Mynheer

45

Tripp. I begged him to be quiet, for things were bad enough without his assistance. Krebs had been hit in the neck by a flying piece of iron and was bleeding like a pig. If he wasn't bandaged, he'd die. Mynheer Tripp plucked at one of his shawls – not offering it, but indicating that, if pressed, he'd part with it. It was filthy enough to have killed Krebs outright: by poisoning. There was nothing for it but to use my shirt; which I did, watched by Mynheer Tripp who snarled when I tore it into strips:

'I hope you know that was your best linen, Vaarlem!'

Which mean remark did nothing but gain me unnecessary thanks from Krebs who could scarcely speak: his wound having severed a tendon and opened a great vessel. He lay in the bottom of the boat while I took the oars, watched by that dirty jelly in the stern. All I could see of Mynheer Tripp were his miserably reproachful eyes.

'You'll die of cold,' he mumbled furiously.

'*I* can keep warm by rowing, sir!' I said, hoping to shame him. I pulled towards the *Little Willelm*'s grave in the frail hope of survivors, but found none. Then, under Kreb's whispered directions, I began to row eastward, into the path of our hoped-for followers on the coming tide. But, being no craftsman of oars, we did little more than drift in that dark and hostile sea: Mynheer Tripp, Krebs and me. For two or even three hours. . . . As Mynheer Tripp had predicted, it was violently cold. I began to shiver and sweat at the same time. My hands were growing very sore and swollen. When I paused to shift my grip, I found them to be bleeding; and Mynheer Tripp, without once stopping, moaned and cursed the sea and the murdering Englishman. Which served no purpose at all. But then he's not the best of companions in such circumstances. He hates the sea and can't abide the sight of blood. Also, there are a million other things capable of panicking him. The chief problem is to avoid being infected by this.

At about one o'clock the breeze began to blow more briskly and in a changed direction. Long bands of cloud began to shift and obscure the moon. The darkness grew thick and formidable; Mynheer Tripp's eyes were no longer visible – but I felt their continuing reproach. Krebs was quite silent and, every now and again, I thought he'd died and had to stop rowing to put my head to his chest and be greeted with: 'Still here . . . don't you worry . . . keep it up, boy –' So back I'd go to my task, abysmally cold and frightened, but not wanting to give the odious Mynheer Tripp the opportunity for gloating.

Then I thought we were saved! Lanterns glinted high up in the night ahead. Our ships at last! I shouted and waved the dim remains of our lantern. Krebs struggled up on his elbow. He said, 'It's the Englishman again!'

'Douse the light, Vaarlem!' shrieked Mynheer Tripp. But it was too late. We'd been seen. The Englishman hailed us.

'Ahoy, there!' Which, in Dutch, means, 'Stand fast or we'll pepper you with musket fire!'

Nearer and nearer she came, a glinting, ghostly monster. Mynheer Tripp began to gabble we'd be tortured and hanged. I never felt more ashamed of him in my life. He was quaking with terror. I sweated to think of how the English would sneer . . . a craven Dutchman. Maybe I could swear he was French: or German? The great ship was alongside. The murderous cannon still poked out of their ports like blunt black teeth against the dark sky. Two English sailors came down on ropes and hoisted Krebs between them. I was surprised by how like Dutchmen they looked. We were bidden to follow, when Mynheer Tripp further disgraced our nation by being frightened of falling off the rope.

'For God's sake, sir!' I hissed at him. 'Make a good showing.'

'What d'you mean, "for God's sake", Vaarlem?' he hissed back. 'You nasty little prig!'

With much contemptuous laughter, more sailors came and helped Mynheer Tripp up between them. I followed on my own. No sooner was I on deck than Mynheer Tripp – who'd got a considerable, jeering crowd about him, shouted in his bad English: 'Cover him up! Boy of good family, that! He'll die of cold!' I flushed angrily, but a huge cloth was brought and wrapped round me. To my indignation, I saw it was an English flag. I stripped it off and flung it down.

'I'd *rather* die of cold than be covered with that!' I meant to display *some* Dutch spirit and show we weren't all like Mynheer Tripp.

'Brave lad!' said an officer – the Captain, I think. 'Worthier than his companion, eh? What say we heave the old fellow back?'

I grew alarmed. Begged them to do no such thing. 'Though you may not think it, he's a great man . . . greater than all of us put together!'

'A greater coward, you mean, boy! How come you go about with such a rag-bag?'

But fortunately, Mynheer Tripp hadn't heard the threat. He was by the mizzen-mast lantern, examining his drawings to see they were intact. A number of officers and sailors were staring over his shoulder. Then more and more came, with more lanterns, lighting up that patch of deck which seemed roofed with canvas and walled by the netted shrouds. Krebs and his honourable wound, and myself and my defiance were left and forgotten. A greater victory was in the making. Of a sudden, I began to feel very proud to be Mynheer Tripp's pupil, and my eyes kept filling with tears on that account. I picked up the flag and wrapped out the cold with it, and went to join the English crowd about my master. Krebs, feeling stronger, leaned on me and stared.

Not all the ships and cannon and defiance in the world could have done what he'd done. With a few lines – no more – he'd advanced into the enemies' hearts and set up his flag there. Mynheer Tripp's victory had been with God's gift – not with the gunsmith's. It's a mercy, I suppose, he never really knew his own power – else he'd have suffocated it under guilders. The Englishmen stared at the drawings, then, seeing Krebs, began comparing with him – in slow English and bad Dutch – the terror and grandeur of their experience, so uncannily caught by the sniffing and shuffling Mynheer Tripp. Pennants, flags, even countries were forgotten. An aspect of battle was seen with neither Dutch nor English eyes, but with a passion and a pity that encompassed all.

'Mynheer Tripp,' said the English Captain – a handsome, well-bred man, most likely of Dutch descent, 'you are a very

48

great man. We are honoured. As our guest, sir, I invite you to visit England.'

My master looked at me – not with pride or any so respectable a thing, but with his usual greed and cunning. He said, in his horrible English, 'Good! Good! I will paint your Admiral, maybe –?'

And then to me in Dutch, with an offensive smirk: 'You see, Vaarlem, these English are different. I told you so. I'll be appreciated – not prosecuted. Just wait till they see what I make of *their* Admiral! Money back, indeed! And after all, my boy, guineas is as good as guilders, eh? He-he!'

He really is the most contemptible man I know! I wonder what the English will make of him: and what he'll make of the English?

The Body-Snatcher

ROBERT LOUIS STEVENSON

Every night in the year, four of us sat in the small parlour of the George at Debenham – the undertaker, and the landlord, and Fettes, and myself. Sometimes there would be more; but blow high, blow low, come rain or snow or frost, we four would be each planted in his own particular armchair. Fettes was an old drunken Scotchman, a man of education obviously, and a man of some property, since he lived in idleness. He had come to Debenham years ago, while still young, and by a mere continuance of living had grown to be an adopted townsman. His blue camlet cloak was a local antiquity, like the church spire. His place in the parlour at the George, his absence from church, his old, crapulous, disreputable vices, were all things of course in Debenham. He had some vague Radical opinions and some fleeting infidelities, which he would now and again set forth and emphasise with tottering slaps upon the table. He drank rum – five glasses regularly every evening; and for the greater portion of his nightly visit to the George sat, with his glass in his right hand, in a state of melancholy alcoholic saturation. We called him the doctor, for he was supposed to have some special knowledge of medicine, and had been known, upon a pinch, to set a fracture or reduce a dislocation; but, beyond these slight particulars, we had no knowledge of his character and antecedents.

One dark winter night – it had struck nine some time before the landlord joined us – there was a sick man in the George, a great neighbouring proprietor suddenly struck down with apoplexy on his way to Parliament; and the great man's still greater London doctor had been telegraphed to his bedside. It was the first time that such a thing had happened in Debenham, for the railway was but newly open, and we were all proportionately moved by the occurrence.

'He's come,' said the landlord, after he had filled and lighted his pipe.

'He?' said I. 'Who? – not the doctor?'

'Himself,' replied our host.

'What is his name?'

'Dr Macfarlane,' said the landlord.

Fettes was far through his third tumbler, stupidly fuddled, now nodding over, now staring mazily around him; but at the last word he seemed to awaken, and repeated the name 'Macfarlane' twice, quietly enough the first time, but with sudden emotion at the second.

'Yes,' said the landlord, 'that's his name, Dr Wolfe Macfarlane.'

Fettes became instantly sober; his eyes awoke, his voice became clear, loud, and steady, his language forcible and earnest. We were all startled by the transformation, as if a man had risen from the dead.

'I beg your pardon,' he said; 'I am afraid I have not been paying much attention to your talk. Who is this Wolfe Macfarlane?' And then, when he had heard the landlord out, 'It cannot be, it cannot be,' he added; 'and yet I would like well to see him face to face.'

'Do you know him, doctor?' asked the undertaker, with a gasp.

'God forbid!' was the reply. 'And yet the name is a strange one; it were too much to fancy two. Tell me, landlord, is he old?'

'Well,' said the host, 'he's not a young man, to be sure, and his hair is white; but he looks younger than you.'

'He is older, though; years older. But,' with a slap upon the table, 'it's the rum you see in my face – rum and sin. This man, perhaps, may have an easy conscience and a good digestion. Conscience! Hear me speak. You would think I was some good, old, decent Christian, would you not? But no, not I; I never canted. Voltaire might have canted if he'd stood in my shoes; but the brains' – with a rattling fillip on his bald head – 'the brains were clear and active, and I saw and made no deductions.'

51

'If you know this doctor,' I ventured to remark, after a somewhat awful pause, 'I should gather that you do not share the landlord's good opinion.'

Fettes paid no regard to me.

'Yes,' he said, with sudden decision, 'I must see him face to face.'

There was another pause, and then a door was closed rather sharply on the first floor, and a step was heard upon the stair.

'That's the doctor,' cried the landlord. 'Look sharp, and you can catch him.'

It was but two steps from the small parlour to the door of the old George Inn; the wide oak staircase landed almost in the street; there was room for a Turkey rug and nothing more between the threshold and the last round of the descent; but this little space was every evening brilliantly lit up, not only by the light upon the stair and the great signal-lamp below the sign, but by the warm radiance of the bar-room window. The George thus brightly advertised itself to passers-by in the cold street. Fettes walked steadily to the spot, and we, who were hanging behind, beheld the two men meet, as one of them had phrased it, face to face. Dr Macfarlane was alert and vigorous. His white hair set off his pale and placid, although energetic, countenance. He was richly dressed in the finest of broadcloth and the whitest of linen, with a great gold watch-chain, and studs and spectacles of the same precious material. He wore a broad-folded tie, white and speckled with lilac, and he carried on his arm a comfortable driving coat of fur. There was no doubt but he became his years, breathing, as he did, of wealth and consideration; and it was a surprising contrast to see our parlour sot – bald, dirty, pimpled, and robed in his old camlet cloak – confront him at the bottom of the stairs.

'Macfarlane!' he said somewhat loudly, more like a herald than a friend.

The great doctor pulled up short on the fourth step, as though the familiarity of the address surprised and somewhat shocked his dignity.

'Toddy Macfarlane!' repeated Fettes.

The London man almost staggered. He stared for the

swiftest of seconds at the man before him, glanced behind him with a sort of scare, and then in a startled whisper, 'Fettes!' he said, 'you!'

'Ay,' said the other, 'me! Did you think I was dead, too? We are not so easy shut of our acquaintance.'

'Hush, hush!' exclaimed the doctor. 'Hush, hush! this meeting is so unexpected – I can see you are unmanned. I hardly knew you, I confess, at first; but I am overjoyed – overjoyed to have this opportunity. For the present it must be how-d'ye-do and good-bye in one, for my fly is waiting, and I must not fail the train; but you shall – let me see – yes – you shall give me your address, and you can count on early news of me. We must do something for you, Fettes. I fear you are out at elbows; but we must see to that for auld lang syne, as once we sang at suppers.'

'Money!' cried Fettes; 'money from you! The money that I had from you is lying where I cast it in the rain.'

Dr Macfarlane had talked himself into some measure of superiority and confidence, but the uncommon energy of this refusal cast him back into his first confusion.

A horrible, ugly look came and went across his almost venerable countenance. 'My dear fellow,' he said, 'be it as you please; my last thought is to offend you. I would intrude on none. I will leave you my address, however –'

'I do not wish it – I do not wish to know the roof that shelters you,' interrupted the other. 'I heard your name; I feared it might be you; I wished to know if, after all, there were a God; I know now that there is none. Begone!'

He still stood in the middle of the rug, between the stair and doorway; and the great London physician, in order to escape, would be forced to step to one side. It was plain that he hesitated before the thought of this humiliation. White as he was, there was a dangerous glitter in his spectacles; but, while he still paused uncertain, he became aware that the driver of his fly was peering in from the street at this unusual scene, and caught a glimpse at the same time of our little body from the parlour, huddled by the corner of the bar. The presence of so many witnesses decided him at once to flee. He crouched together, brushing on the wainscot, and made a dart like a serpent, striking for the door. But his tribulation was not yet entirely at an end, for even as he was passing Fettes clutched him by the arm and these words came in a whisper, and yet painfully distinct, 'Have you seen it again?'

The great rich London doctor cried out aloud with a sharp, throttling cry; he dashed his questioner across the open space, and, with his hands over his head, fled out of the door like a detected thief. Before it had occurred to one of us to make a movement the fly was already rattling toward the station. The scene was over like a dream, but the dream had left proofs and traces of its passage. Next day the servant found the fine gold spectacles broken on the threshold, and that very night we were all standing breathless by the bar-room window, and Fettes at our side, sober, pale, and resolute in look.

'God protect us, Mr Fettes!' said the landlord, coming first into possession of his customary senses. 'What in the universe is all this? These are strange things you have been saying.'

Fettes turned toward us; he looked us each in succession in the face. 'See if you can hold your tongues,' said he. 'That man Macfarlane is not safe to cross; those that have done so already have repented it too late.'

And then, without so much as finishing his third glass, far less waiting for the other two, he bade us good-bye and went forth, under the lamp of the hotel, into the black night.

We three turned to our places in the parlour, with the big red fire and four clear candles; and, as we recapitulated what had passed, the first chill of our surprise soon changed into a glow of curiosity. We sat late; it was the latest session I have known in the old George. Each man, before we parted, had his theory that he was bound to prove; and none of us had any nearer business in this world than to track out the past of our condemned companion, and surprise the secret that he shared with the great London doctor. It is no great boast, but I believe I was a better hand at worming out a story than either of my fellows at the George; and perhaps there is now no other man alive who could narrate to you the following foul and unnatural events.

In his young days Fettes studied medicine in the schools of Edinburgh. He had talent of a kind, the talent that picks up swiftly what it hears and readily retails it for its own. He worked little at home; but he was civil, attentive, and intelligent in the presence of his masters. They soon picked him out as a lad who listened closely and remembered well; nay, strange as it seemed to me when I first heard it, he was in those days well favoured, and pleased by his exterior. There was, at that period, a certain extramural teacher of anatomy, whom I shall here designate by the letter K. His name was subsequently too well known. The man who bore it skulked through the streets of Edinburgh in disguise, while the mob that applauded at the execution of Burke called loudly for the blood of his employer. But Mr K—— was then at the top of his vogue; he enjoyed a popularity due partly to his own talent and address, partly to the incapacity of his rival, the university professor. The students, at least, swore by his name, and Fettes believed himself, and was believed by others, to have laid the foundations of success when he had acquired the favour of this meteorically famous man. Mr K—— was a *bon vivant* as well as an accomplished teacher; he liked a sly illusion no less than a careful preparation. In both capacities Fettes enjoyed and deserved his notice, and by the second year of his attendance he held the half-regular position of second demonstrator or sub-assistant in his class.

In this capacity the charge of the theatre and lecture-room devolved in particular upon his shoulders. He had to answer for the cleanliness of the premises and the conduct of the other students, and it was a part of his duty to supply, receive, and divide the various subjects. It was with a view to this last – at that time very delicate – affair that he was lodged by Mr K—— in the same wynd, and at last in the same building, with the dissecting-rooms. Here, after a night of turbulent pleasures, his hand still tottering, his sight still misty and confused, he would be called out of bed in the black hours before the winter dawn by the unclean and desperate interlopers who supplied the table. He would open the door to these men, since infamous throughout the land. He would help them with their

55

tragic burden, pay them their sordid price, and remain alone, when they were gone, with the unfriendly relics of humanity. From such a scene he would return to snatch another hour or two of slumber, to repair the abuses of the night, and refresh himself for the labours of the day.

Few lads could have been more insensible to the impressions of a life thus passed among the ensigns of mortality. His mind was closed against all general considerations. He was incapable of interest in the fate and fortunes of another, the slave of his own desires and low ambitions. Cold, light, and selfish in the last resort, he had that modicum of prudence, miscalled morality, which keeps a man from inconvenient drunkenness or punishable theft. He coveted, besides, a measure of consideration from his masters and his fellow-pupils, and he had no desire to fail conspicuously in the external parts of life. Thus he made it his pleasure to gain some distinction in his studies, and day after day rendered unimpeachable eye-service to his employer, Mr K——. For his day of work he indemnified himself by nights of roaring, blackguardly enjoyment; and when that balance had been struck, the organ that he called his conscience declared itself content.

The supply of subjects was a continual trouble to him as well as to his master. In that large and busy class, the raw material of the anatomists kept perpetually running out; and the business thus rendered necessary was not only unpleasant in itself, but threatened dangerous consequences to all who were concerned. It was the policy of Mr K—— to ask no questions in his dealings with the trade. 'They bring the body, and we pay the price,' he used to say, dwelling on the alliteration – '*quid pro quo*.' And, again, and somewhat profanely, 'Ask no questions,' he would tell his assistants, 'for conscience' sake.' There was no understanding that the subjects were provided by the crime of murder. Had that idea been broached to him in words, he would have recoiled in horror; but the lightness of his speech upon so grave a matter was, in itself, an offence against good manners, and a temptation to the men with whom he dealt. Fettes, for instance, had often remarked to himself upon the singular freshness of the bodies. He had been struck again and again by the hangdog, abominable looks of the ruffians who came to him before the dawn; and, putting things together clearly in his private thoughts, he perhaps attributed a meaning too immoral and too categorical to the unguarded counsels of his master. He understood his duty, in short, to have three branches: to take what was brought, to pay the price, and to avert the eye from any evidence of crime.

One November morning this policy of silence was put sharply to the test. He had been awake all night with a racking toothache – pacing his room like a caged beast or throwing himself in fury on his bed – and had fallen at last into that profound, uneasy slumber that so often follows on a night of pain, when he was awakened by the third or fourth angry repetition of the concerted signal. There was a thin, bright moonshine; it was bitter cold, windy, and frosty; the town had not yet awakened, but an indefinable stir already preluded the noise and business of the day. The ghouls had come later than usual, and they seemed more than usually eager to be gone. Fettes, sick with sleep, lighted them upstairs. He heard their grumbling Irish voices through a dream; and as they stripped the sack from their sad merchandise he leaned dozing, with his shoulder propped against the wall; he had to shake himself to find the men their money. As he did so his eyes lighted on the dead face. He started; he took two steps nearer, with the candle raised.

'God Almighty!' he cried. 'That is Jane Galbraith!'

The men answered nothing, but they shuffled nearer the door.

'I know her, I tell you,' he continued. 'She was alive and hearty yesterday. It's impossible she can be dead; it's impossible you should have got this body fairly.'

'Sure, sir, you're mistaken entirely,' said one of the men.

But the other looked Fettes darkly in the eyes, and demanded the money on the spot.

It was impossible to misconceive the threat or to exaggerate the danger. The lad's heart failed him. He stammered some excuses, counted out the sum, and saw his hateful visitors depart. No sooner were they gone than he hastened to confirm his doubts. By a dozen unquestionable marks he identified the girl he had jested with the day before. He saw, with horror, marks upon her body that might well betoken violence. A panic seized him, and he took refuge in his room. There he reflected at length over the discovery that he had made; considered soberly the bearing of Mr K——'s instructions and the danger to himself of interference in so serious a business, and at last, in sore perplexity, determined to wait for the advice of his immediate superior, the class assistant.

This was a young doctor, Wolfe Macfarlane, a high favourite among all the reckless students, clever, dissipated, and unscrupulous to the last degree. He had travelled and studied abroad. His manners were agreeable and a little forward. He was an authority on the stage, skilful on the ice or the links with skate or golf-club; he dressed with nice audacity, and, to put the finishing touch upon his glory, he kept a gig and a strong trotting-horse. With Fettes he was on terms of intimacy; indeed, their relative positions called for some community of life; and when subjects were scarce the pair would drive far into the country in Macfarlane's gig, visit and desecrate some lonely graveyard, and return before dawn with their booty to the door of the dissecting-room.

On that particular morning Macfarlane arrived somewhat earlier than his wont. Fettes heard him, and met him on the stairs, told him his story, and showed him the cause of his alarm. Macfarlane examined the marks on her body.

'Yes,' he said with a nod, 'it looks fishy.'

'Well, what should I do?' asked Fettes.

'Do?' repeated the other. 'Do you want to do anything? Least said soonest mended, I should say.'

'Some one else might recognise her,' objected Fettes. 'She was as well known as the Castle Rock.'

'We'll hope not,' said Macfarlane, 'and if anybody does – well, you didn't, don't you see, and there's an end. The fact is, this has been going on too long. Stir up the mud, and you'll get K—— into the most unholy trouble; you'll be in a shocking box yourself. So will I, if you come to that. I should like to know how any one of us would look, or what the devil we

58

should have to say for ourselves, in any Christian witness-box. For me, you know, there's one thing certain – that, practically speaking, all our subjects have been murdered.'

'Macfarlane!' cried Fettes.

'Come now!' sneered the other. 'As if you hadn't suspected it yourself!'

'Suspecting is one thing –'

'And proof another. Yes, I know; and I'm as sorry as you are this should have come here,' tapping the body with his cane. 'The next best thing for me is not to recognize it; and,' he added coolly, 'I don't. You may, if you please. I don't dictate, but I think a man of the world would do as I do; and, I may add, I fancy that is what K—— would look for at our hands. The question is, Why did he choose us two for his assistants? And I answer, Because he didn't want old wives.'

This was the tone of all others to affect the mind of a lad like Fettes. He agreed to imitate Macfarlane. The body of the unfortunate girl was duly dissected, and no one remarked or appeared to recognize her.

One afternoon, when his day's work was over, Fettes dropped into a popular tavern and found Macfarlane sitting with a stranger. This was a small man, very pale and dark, with coal-black eyes. The cut of his features gave a promise of intellect and refinement which was but feebly realized in his manners, for he proved, upon a nearer acquaintance, coarse, vulgar, and stupid. He exercised, however, a very remarkable control over Macfarlane; issued orders like the Great Bashaw; became inflamed at the least discussion or delay, and commented rudely on the servility with which he was obeyed. This most offensive person took a fancy to Fettes on the spot, plied him with drinks, and honoured him with unusual confidences on his past career. If a tenth part of what he confessed were true, he was a very loathsome rogue; and the lad's vanity was tickled by the attention of so experienced a man.

'I'm a pretty bad fellow myself,' the stranger remarked, 'but Macfarlane is the boy – Toddy Macfarlane I call him. Toddy, order your friend another glass.' Or it might be, 'Toddy, you jump up and shut the door.' 'Toddy hates me,' he said again. 'Oh, yes, Toddy, you do!'

'Don't you call me that confounded name,' growled Macfarlane.

'Hear him! Did you ever see the lads play knife? He would like to do that all over my body,' remarked the stranger.

'We medicals have a better way than that,' said Fettes. 'When we dislike a dead friend of ours, we dissect him.'

Macfarlane looked up sharply, as though this jest were scarcely to his mind.

The afternoon passed. Gray, for that was the stranger's name, invited Fettes to join them at dinner, ordered a feast so sumptuous that the tavern was thrown into commotion, and when all was done commanded Macfarlane to settle the bill. It was late before they separated; the man Gray was incapably drunk. Macfarlane, sobered by his fury, chewed the cud of the money he had been forced to squander and the slights he had been obliged to swallow. Fettes, with various liquors singing in his head, returned home with devious footsteps and a mind entirely in abeyance. Next day Macfarlane was absent from the class, and Fettes smiled to himself as he imagined him still squiring the intolerable Gray from tavern to tavern. As soon as the hour of liberty had struck, he posted from place to place in quest of his last night's companions. He could find them, however, nowhere; so returned early to his rooms, went early to bed, and slept the sleep of the just.

At four in the morning he was awakened by the well-known signal. Descending to the door, he was filled with astonishment to find Macfarlane with his gig, and in the gig one of those long and ghastly packages with which he was so well acquainted.

'What?' he cried. 'Have you been out alone? How did you manage?'

But Macfarlane silenced him roughly, bidding him turn to business. When they had got the body upstairs and laid it on the table, Macfarlane made at first as if he were going away. Then he paused and seemed to hesitate; and then, 'You had better look at the face,' said he, in tones of some constraint.

60

'You had better,' he repeated, as Fettes only stared at him in wonder.

'But where, and how, and when did you come by it?' cried the other.

'Look at the face,' was the only answer.

Fettes was staggered; strange doubts assailed him. He looked from the young doctor to the body, and then back again. At last, with a start, he did as he was bidden. He had almost expected the sight that met his eyes, and yet the shock was cruel. To see, fixed in the rigidity of death and naked on that coarse layer of sackcloth, the man whom he had left well clad and full of meat and sin upon the threshold of a tavern, awoke, even in the thoughtless Fettes, some of the terrors of the conscience. It was a *cras tibi* which re-echoed in his soul, that two whom he had known should have come to lie upon these icy tables. Yet these were only secondary thoughts. His first concern regarded Wolfe. Unprepared for a challenge so momentous, he knew not how to look his comrade in the face. He durst not meet his eye, and he had neither words nor voice at his command.

It was Macfarlane himself who made the first advance. He came up quietly behind and laid his hand gently but firmly on the other's shoulder.

'Richardson,' said he, 'may have the head.'

Now, Richardson was a student who had long been anxious for that portion of the human subject to dissect. There was no answer, and the murderer resumed: 'Talking of business, you must pay me; your accounts, you see, must tally.'

Fettes found a voice, the ghost of his own: 'Pay you!' he cried. 'Pay you for that?'

'Why, yes, of course you must. By all means and on every possible account, you must,' returned the other. 'I dare not give it for nothing, you dare not take it for nothing; it would compromise us both. This is another case like Jane Galbraith's. The more things are wrong, the more we must act as if all were right. Where does old K—— keep his money?'

'There,' answered Fettes hoarsely, pointing to a cupboard in the corner.

'Give me the key, then,' said the other calmly, holding out his hand.

There was an instant's hesitation, and the die was cast. Macfarlane could not suppress a nervous twitch, the infinitesimal mark of an immense relief, as he felt the key between his fingers. He opened the cupboard, brought out pen and ink and a paper-book that stood in one compartment, and separated from the funds in a drawer a sum suitable to the occasion.

'Now, look here,' he said, 'there is the payment made – first proof of your good faith: first step to your security. You have now to clinch it by a second. Enter the payment in your book, and then you for your part may defy the devil.'

The next few seconds were for Fettes an agony of thought; but in balancing his terrors it was the most immediate that triumphed. Any future difficulty seemed almost welcome if he could avoid a present quarrel with Macfarlane. He set down the candle which he had been carrying all this time, and with a steady hand entered the date, the nature, and the amount of the transaction.

'And now,' said Macfarlane, 'it's only fair that you should pocket the lucre. I've had my share already. By the by, when a man of the world falls into a bit of luck, has a few shillings extra in his pocket – I'm ashamed to speak of it, but there's a rule of conduct in the case. No treating, no purchase of expensive class-books, no squaring of old debts; borrow, don't lend.'

'Macfarlane,' began Fettes, still somewhat hoarsely, 'I have put my neck in a halter to oblige you.'

'To oblige me?' cried Wolfe. 'Oh come! You did, as near as I can see the matter, what you downright had to do in self-defence. Suppose I got into trouble, where would you be? This second little matter flows clearly from the first. Mr Gray is the continuation of Miss Galbraith. You can't begin and then stop. If you begin, you must keep on beginning; that's the truth. No rest for the wicked.'

A horrible sense of blackness and the treachery of fate seized hold upon the soul of the unhappy student.

'My God!' he cried, 'but what have I done? and when did I begin? To be made a class assistant – in the name of reason, where's the harm in that? Service wanted the position; Service might have got it. Would *he* have been where *I* am now?'

'My dear fellow,' said Macfarlane, 'what a boy you are! What harm *has* come to you? What harm *can* come to you if you hold your tongue? Why, man, do you know what this life is? There are two squads of us – the lions and the lambs. If you're a lamb, you'll come to lie upon these tables like Gray or Jane Galbraith; if you're a lion, you'll live and drive a horse like me, like K——, like all the world with any wit or courage. You're staggered at the first. But look at K——! My dear fellow, you're clever, you have pluck. I like you, and K—— likes you. You were born to lead the hunt; and I tell you, on my honour and my experience of life, three days from now you'll laugh at all these scarecrows like a High School boy at a farce.'

And with that Macfarlane took his departure and drove off up the wynd in his gig to get under cover before daylight. Fettes was thus left alone with his regrets. He saw the miserable peril in which he stood involved. He saw, with inexpressible dismay, that there was no limit to his weakness, and that, from concession to concession, he had fallen from the arbiter of Macfarlane's destiny to his paid and helpless accomplice. He would have given the world to have been a little braver at the time, but it did not occur to him that he might still be brave. The secret of Jane Galbraith and the cursed entry in the daybook closed his mouth.

Hours passed; the class began to arrive; the members of the unhappy Gray were dealt out to one and to another, and received without remark. Richardson was made happy with the head; and, before the hour of freedom rang, Fettes trembled with exultation to perceive how far they had already gone toward safety.

For two days he continued to watch, with an increasing joy, the dreadful process of disguise.

On the third day Macfarlane made his appearance. He had been ill, he said; but he made up for lost time by the energy with which he directed the students. To Richardson in particular he extended the most valuable assistance and advice, and that student, encouraged by the praise of the demonstrator, burned high with ambitious hopes, and saw the medal already in his grasp.

Before the week was out Macfarlane's prophecy had been fulfilled. Fettes had outlived his terrors and had forgotten his baseness. He began to plume himself upon his courage, and had so arranged the story in his mind that he could look back on these events with an unhealthy pride. Of his accomplice he saw but little. They met, of course, in the business of the class; they received their orders together from Mr K——. At times they had a word or two in private, and Macfarlane was from first to last particularly kind and jovial. But it was plain that he avoided any reference to their common secret; and even when Fettes whispered to him that he had cast in his lot with the lions and forsworn the lambs, he only signed to him smilingly to hold his peace.

At length an occasion arose which threw the pair once more into a closer union. Mr K—— was again short of subjects; pupils were eager, and it was a part of this teacher's pretensions to be always well supplied. At the same time there came the news of a burial in the rustic graveyard of Glencorse. Time has little changed the place in question. It stood then, as now, upon a cross-road, out of call of human habitations, and buried fathom deep in the foliage of six cedar-trees. The cries of the sheep upon the neighbouring hills, the streamlets upon either hand, one loudly singing among pebbles, the other dripping furtively from pond to pond, the stir of the wind in mountainous old flowering chestnuts, and once in seven days the voice of the bell and the old tunes of the precentor, were the only sounds that disturbed the silence around the rural church. The Resurrection Man – to use a byname of the period – was not to be deterred by any of the sanctities of customary piety. It was part of his trade to despise and desecrate the scrolls and trumpets of old tombs, the paths worn by the feet of worshippers and mourners, and the offerings and the inscriptions of bereaved affection. To rustic neighbourhoods where love is more than commonly tenacious, and where some bonds of blood or fellowship unite the entire society of a parish, the

body-snatcher, far from being repelled by natural respect, was attracted by the ease and safety of the task. To bodies that had been laid in earth, in joyful expectation of a far different awakening, there came that hasty, lamp-lit, terror-haunted resurrection of the spade and mattock. The coffin was forced, the cerements torn, and the melancholy relics, clad in sackcloth, after being rattled for hours on moonless by-ways, were at length exposed to uttermost indignities before a class of gaping boys.

Somewhat as two vultures may swoop upon a dying lamb, Fettes and Macfarlane were to be let loose upon a grave in that green and quiet resting-place. The wife of a farmer, a woman who had lived for sixty years, and been known for nothing but good butter and a godly conversation, was to be rooted from her grave at midnight and carried, dead and naked, to that far-away city that she had always honoured with her Sunday's best; the place beside her family was to be empty till the crack of doom, her innocent and almost venerable members to be exposed to that last curiosity of the anatomist.

Late one afternoon the pair set forth, well wrapped in cloaks and furnished with a formidable bottle. It rained without remission – a cold, dense, lashing rain. Now and again there blew a puff of wind, but these sheets of falling water kept it down. Bottle and all, it was a sad and silent drive as far as Penicuik, where they were to spend the evening. They stopped once, to hide their implements in a thick bush not far from the churchyard, and once again at the Fisher's Tryst, to have a toast before the kitchen fire and vary their nips of whisky with a glass of ale. When they reached their journey's end the gig was housed, the horse was fed and comforted, and the two young doctors in a private room sat down to the best dinner and the best wine the house afforded. The lights, the fire, the beating rain upon the window, the cold, incongruous work that lay before them, added zest to their enjoyment of the meal. With every glass their cordiality increased. Soon Macfarlane handed a little pile of gold to his companion.

'A compliment,' he said. 'Between friends these little d——d accommodations ought to fly like pipe-lights.'

Fettes pocketed the money, and applauded the sentiment to the echo. 'You are a philosopher,' he cried. 'I was an ass till I knew you. You and K—— between you, by the Lord Harry! but you'll make a man of me.'

'Of course we shall,' applauded Macfarlane. 'A man? I tell you, it required a man to back me up the other morning. There are some big, brawling, forty-year-old cowards who would have turned sick at the look of the d——d thing; but not you – you kept your head. I watched you.'

'Well, and why not?' Fettes thus vaunted himself. 'It was no affair of mine. There was nothing to gain on the one side but disturbance, and on the other I could count on your gratitude, don't you see?' And he slapped his pocket till the gold pieces rang.

Macfarlane somehow felt a certain touch of alarm at these unpleasant words. He may have regretted that he had taught his young companion so successfully, but he had no time to interfere, for the other noisily continued in this boastful strain:

'The great thing is not to be afraid. Now, between you and me, I don't want to hang – that's practical; but for all cant, Macfarlane, I was born with a contempt. Hell, God, devil, right, wrong, sin, crime, and all the old gallery of curiosities – they may frighten boys, but men of the world, like you and me, despise them. Here's to the memory of Gray!'

It was by this time growing somewhat late. The gig, according to order, was brought round to the door with both lamps brightly shining, and the young men had to pay their bill and take the road. They announced that they were bound for Peebles, and drove in that direction till they were clear of the last houses of the town; then, extinguishing the lamps, returned upon their course, and followed a by-road toward Glencorse. There was no sound but that of their own passage, and the incessant, strident pouring of the rain. It was pitch dark; here and there a white gate or a white stone in the wall guided them for a short space across the night; but for the most part it was at a foot pace, and almost groping, that they picked their way through that resonant blackness to their solemn and isolated destination. In the sunken woods that traverse the neighbourhood of the burying-ground the last glimmer failed them, and it became necessary to kindle a match and re-illumine one of the lanterns of the gig. Thus, under the dripping trees, and environed by huge and moving shadows, they reached the scene of their unhallowed labours.

They were both experienced in such affairs, and powerful with the spade; and they had scarce been twenty minutes at their task before they were rewarded by a dull rattle on the coffin-lid. At the same moment, Macfarlane, having hurt his hand upon a stone, flung it carelessly above his head. The grave, in which they now stood almost to the shoulders, was close to the edge of the plateau of the graveyard; and the gig lamp had been propped, the better to illuminate their labours, against a tree, and on the immediate verge of the steep bank descending to the stream. Chance had taken a sure aim with the stone. Then came a clang of broken glass; night fell upon them; sounds alternately dull and ringing announced the bounding of the lantern down the bank, and its occasional collision with the trees. A stone or two, which it had dislodged in its descent, rattled behind it into the profundities of the glen; and then silence, like night, resumed its sway; and they might bend their hearing to its utmost pitch, but naught was to be heard except the rain, now marching to the wind, now steadily falling over miles of open country.

They were so nearly at an end of their abhorred task that they judged it wisest to complete it in the dark. The coffin was exhumed and broken open; the body inserted in the dripping sack and carried between them to the gig; one mounted to keep it in its place, and the other, taking the horse by the mouth, groped along by wall and bush until they reached the wider road by the Fisher's Tryst. Here was a faint, diffused radiancy, which they hailed like daylight; by that they pushed the horse to a good pace and began to rattle along merrily in the direction of the town.

They had both been wetted to the skin during their operations, and now, as the gig jumped among the deep ruts, the thing that stood propped between them fell now upon one and now upon the other. At every repetition of the horrid contact each instinctively repelled it with the greater haste; and the process, natural although it was, began to tell upon the nerves of the companions. Macfarlane made some ill-favoured jest about the farmer's wife, but it came hollowly from his lips, and was allowed to drop in silence. Still their unnatural burden bumped from side to side; and now the head would be laid, as if in confidence, upon their shoulders, and now the drenching sack-cloth would flap icily about their faces. A creeping chill began to possess the soul of Fettes. He peered at the bundle, and it seemed somehow larger than at first. All over the country-side, and from every degree of distance, the farm dogs accompanied their passage with tragic ululations; and it grew and grew upon his mind that some unnatural miracle had been accomplished, that some nameless change had befallen the dead body, and that it was in fear of their unholy burden that the dogs were howling.

'For God's sake,' said he, making a great effort to arrive at speech, 'for God's sake, let's have a light!'

Seemingly Macfarlane was affected in the same direction; for, though he made no reply, he stopped the horse, passed the reins to his companion, got down, and proceeded to kindle the remaining lamp. They had by that time got no farther than the cross-road down to Auchenclinny. The rain still poured as though the deluge were returning, and it was no easy matter to make a light in such a world of wet and darkness. When at last the flickering blue flame had been transferred to the wick and began to expand and clarify, and shed a wide circle of misty brightness round the gig, it became possible for the two young men to see each other and the thing they had along with them. The rain had moulded the rough sacking to the outlines of the body underneath; the head was distinct from the trunk, the shoulders plainly modelled; something at once spectral and human riveted their eyes upon the ghastly comrade of their drive.

For some time Macfarlane stood motionless, holding up the lamp. A nameless dread was swathed, like a wet sheet, about the body, and tightened the white skin upon the face of Fettes; a fear that was meaningless, a horror of what could not be, kept mounting to his brain. Another beat of the watch, and he had spoken. But his comrade forestalled him.

'That is not a woman,' said Macfarlane, in a hushed voice.

'It was a woman when we put her in,' whispered Fettes.

'Hold that lamp,' said the other. 'I must see her face.'

And as Fettes took the lamp his companion untied the fastenings of the sack and drew down the cover from the head. The light fell very clear upon the dark, well-moulded features and smooth-shaven cheeks of a too familiar countenance, often beheld in dreams of both of these young men. A wild yell rang up into the night; each leaped from his own side into the roadway: the lamp fell, broke, and was extinguished; and the horse, terrified by this unusual commotion, bounded and went off toward Edinburgh at a gallop, bearing along with it, sole occupant of the gig, the body of the dead and long-dissected Gray.

The Doll's Ghost

F. MARION CRAWFORD

It was a terrible accident, and for one moment the splendid
machinery of Cranston House got out of gear and stood still.
The butler emerged from the retirement in which he spent his
elegant leisure, two grooms of the chambers appeared simul-
taneously from opposite directions, there were actually house-
maids on the grand staircase, and those who remember the
facts most exactly assert that Mrs Pringle herself positively
stood upon the landing. Mrs Pringle was the housekeeper. As
for the head nurse, the under nurse, and the nursery-maid,
their feelings cannot be described.

The Lady Gwendolen Lancaster-Douglas-Scroop, youngest
daughter of the ninth Duke of Cranston, and aged six years
and three months, picked herself up quite alone, and sat down
on the third step of the grand staircase in Cranston House.

'Oh!' ejaculated the butler, and he disappeared again.

'Ah!' responded the grooms of the chambers, as they also
went away.

'It's only that doll,' Mrs Pringle was distinctly heard to say,
in a tone of contempt.

The under nurse heard her say it. Then the three nurses
gathered round Lady Gwendolen and patted her, and gave her
unhealthy things out of their pockets, and hurried her out of
Cranston House as fast as they could, lest it should be found
out upstairs that they had allowed the Lady Gwendolen
Lancaster-Douglas-Scroop to tumble down the grand staircase
with her doll in her arms. And as the doll was badly broken,
the nursery-maid carried it, with the pieces, wrapped up in
Lady Gwendolen's little cloak. It was not far to Hyde Park,
and when they had reached a quiet place they took means to
find out that Lady Gwendolen had no bruises. For the carpet

71

was very thick and soft, and there was thick stuff under it to make it softer.

Lady Gwendolen Douglas-Scroop sometimes yelled, but she never cried. It was because she had yelled that the nurse had allowed her to go downstairs alone with Nina, the doll, under one arm, while she steadied herself with her other hand on the balustrade, and trod upon the polished marble steps beyond the edge of the carpet. So she had fallen, and Nina had come to grief . . .

Mr Bernard Puckler and his little daughter lived in a little house in a little alley, which led out off a quiet little street not very far from Belgrave Square. He was the great doll doctor, and his extensive practice lay in the most aristocratic quarter. He mended dolls of all sizes and ages, boy dolls and girl dolls, baby dolls in long clothes, and grown-up dolls in fashionable gowns, talking dolls and dumb dolls, those that shut their eyes when they lay down, and those whose eyes had to be shut for them by means of a mysterious wire. His daughter Else was only just over twelve years old, but she was already very clever at mending dolls' clothes, and at doing their hair, which is harder than you might think, though the dolls sit quite still while it is being done.

Mr Puckler had originally been a German, but he had dissolved his nationality in the ocean of London many years ago, like a great many foreigners. He still had one or two German friends, however, who came on Saturday evenings and smoked with him and played picquet or 'skat' with him for farthing points, and called him 'Herr Doctor', which seemed to please Mr Puckler very much.

He looked older than he was, for his beard was rather long and ragged, his hair was grizzled and thin, and he wore horn-rimmed spectacles.

As for Else, she was a thin, pale child, very quiet and neat, with dark eyes and brown hair that was plaited down her back and tied with a bit of black ribbon. She mended the dolls' clothes and took the dolls back to their homes when they were quite strong again.

The house was a little one, but too big for the two people

who lived in it. There was a small sitting-room on the street, and the workshop was at the back, and there were three rooms upstairs. But the father and daughter lived most of their time in the workshop, because they were generally at work, even in the evenings.

Mr Puckler laid Nina on the table and looked at her a long time, till the tears began to fill his eyes behind the horn-rimmed spectacles. He was a very susceptible man, and he often fell in love with the dolls he mended, and found it hard to part with them when they had smiled at him for a few days. They were real little people to him, with characters and thoughts and feelings of their own, and he was very tender with them all. But some attracted him especially from the first, and when they were brought to him maimed and injured, their state seemed so pitiful to him that the tears came easily. You must remember that he had lived among dolls during a great part of his life, and understood them.

'How do you know that they feel nothing?' he went on to say to Else. 'You must be gentle with them. It costs nothing to be kind to the little beings, and perhaps it makes a difference to them.'

And Else understood him, because she was a child, and she knew that she was more to him than all the dolls.

He fell in love with Nina at first sight, perhaps because her beautiful brown glass eyes were something like Else's own, and he loved Else first and best, with all his heart. And, besides, it was a very sorrowful case. Nina had evidently not been long in the world, for her complexion was perfect, her hair was smooth where it should be smooth, and curly where it should be curly, and her silk clothes were perfectly new. But across her face was that frightful gash, like a sabre-cut, deep and shadowy within, but clean and sharp at the edges. When he tenderly pressed her head to close the gaping wound, the edges made a fine, grating sound that was painful to hear, and the lids of the dark eyes quivered and trembled as though Nina were suffering dreadfully.

'Poor Nina!' he exclaimed sorrowfully. 'But I shall not hurt you much, though you will take a long time to get strong.'

He always asked the names of the broken dolls when they were brought to him, and sometimes the people knew what the children called them, and told him. He liked 'Nina' for a name. Altogether and in every way she pleased him more than any doll he had seen for many years, and he felt drawn to her, and made up his mind to make her perfectly strong and sound, no matter how much labour it might cost him.

Mr Puckler worked patiently a little at a time, and Else watched him. She could do nothing for poor Nina, whose clothes needed no mending. The longer the doll doctor worked the more fond he became of the yellow hair and the beautiful brown glass eyes. He sometimes forgot all the other dolls that were waiting to be mended, lying side by side on a shelf, and sat for an hour gazing at Nina's face, while he racked his ingenuity for some new invention by which to hide even the smallest trace of the terrible accident.

She was wonderfully mended. Even he was obliged to admit that; but the scar was still visible to his keen eyes, a very fine line right across the face, downwards from right to left. Yet all the conditions had been most favourable for a cure, since the cement had set quite hard at the first attempt and the weather had been fine and dry, which makes a great difference in a dolls' hospital.

At last he knew that he could do no more, and the under nurse had already come twice to see whether the job was finished, as she coarsely expressed it.

'Nina is not quite strong yet,' Mr Puckler had answered each time, for he could not make up his mind to face the parting.

And now he sat before the square deal table at which he worked, and Nina lay before him for the last time with a big brown-paper box beside her. It stood there like her coffin, waiting for her, he thought. He must put her into it, and lay tissue paper over her dear face, and then put on the lid, and at the thought of tying the string his sight was dim with tears again. He was never to look into the glassy depths of the beautiful brown eyes any more, nor to hear the little wooden voice say 'Pa-pa' and 'Ma-ma'. It was a very painful moment.

74

In the vain hope of gaining time before the separation, he took up the little sticky bottles of cement and glue and gum and colour, looking at each one in turn, and then at Nina's face. And all his small tools lay there, neatly arranged in a row, but he knew that he could not use them again for Nina. She was quite strong at last, and in a country where there should be no cruel children to hurt her she might live a hundred years, with only that almost imperceptible line across her face, to tell of the fearful thing that had befallen her on the marble steps of Cranston House.

Suddenly Mr Puckler's heart was quite full, and he rose abruptly from his seat and turned away.

'Else,' he said unsteadily, 'you must do it for me. I cannot bear to see her go into the box.'

So he went and stood at the window with his back turned, while Else did what he had not the heart to do.

'Is it done?' he asked, not turning round. 'Then take her away, my dear. Put on your hat, and take her to Cranston House quickly, and when you are gone I will turn round.'

Else was used to her father's queer ways with the dolls, and though she had never seen him so much moved by a parting, she was not much surprised.

'Come back quickly,' he said, when he heard her hand on the latch. 'It is growing late, and I should not send you at this hour. But I cannot bear to look forward to it any more.'

When Else was gone, he left the window and sat down in his place before the table again, to wait for the child to come back. He touched the place where Nina had lain, very gently, and he recalled the softly-tinted pink face, and the glass eyes, and the ringlets of yellow hair, till he could almost see them.

The evenings were long, for it was late in the spring. But it began to grow dark soon, and Mr Puckler wondered why Else did not come back. She had been gone an hour and a half, and that was much longer than he had expected, for it was barely half a mile from Belgrave Square to Cranston House. He reflected that the child might have been kept waiting, but as the twilight deepened he grew anxious, and walked up and

75

down in the dim workshop, no longer thinking of Nina, but of Else, his own living child, whom he loved.

An indefinable, disquieting sensation came upon him by fine degrees, a chilliness and a faint stirring of his thin hair, joined with a wish to be in any company rather than to be alone much longer. It was the beginning of fear.

He told himself in strong German-English that he was a foolish old man, and he began to feel about for the matches in the dusk. He knew just where they should be, for he always kept them in the same place, close to the little tin box that held bits of sealing-wax of various colours, for some kinds of mending. But somehow he could not find the matches in the gloom.

Something had happened to Else, he was sure, and as his fear increased, he felt as though it might be allayed if he could get a light and see what time it was. Then he called himself a foolish old man again, and the sound of his own voice startled him in the dark. He could not find the matches.

The window was grey still; he might see what time it was if he went close to it, and he could go and get matches out of the cupboard afterwards. He stood back from the table, to get out of the way of the chair, and began to cross the board floor.

Something was following him in the dark. There was a small pattering, as of tiny feet upon the boards. He stopped and listened, and the roots of his hair tingled. It was nothing and he was a foolish old man. He made two steps more, and he was sure that he heard the little pattering again. He turned his back to the window, leaning against the sash so that the panes began to crack, and he faced the dark. Everything was quite still, and it smelt of paste and cement and wood-filings as usual.

'Is that you, Else?' he asked, and he was surprised by the fear in his voice.

There was no answer in the room, and he held up his watch and tried to make out what time it was by the grey dusk that was just not darkness. So far as he could see, it was within two or three minutes of ten o'clock. He had been a long time alone. He was shocked, and frightened for Else, out in London, so

76

late, and he almost ran across the room to the door. As he fumbled for the latch, he distinctly heard the running of the little feet after him.

'Mice!' he exclaimed feebly, just as he got the door open.

He shut it quickly behind him, and felt as though some cold thing had settled on his back and were writhing upon him. The passage was quite dark, but he found his hat and was out in the alley in a moment, breathing more freely, and surprised to find how much light there still was in the open air. He could see the pavement clearly under his feet, and far off in the street to which the alley led he could hear the laughter and calls of children, playing some game out of doors. He wondered how he could have been so nervous, and for an instant he thought of going back into the house to wait quietly for Else. But instantly he felt that nervous fright of something stealing over him again. In any case it was better to walk up to Cranston House and ask the servants about the child. One of the women had perhaps taken a fancy to her, and was even now giving her tea and cake.

He walked quickly to Belgrave Square, and then up the broad streets, listening as he went, whenever there was no other sound, for the tiny footsteps. But he heard nothing, and was laughing at himself when he rang the servants' bell at the big house. Of course, the child must be there.

The person who opened the door was quite an inferior person – for it was a back door – but affected the manners of the front, and stared at Mr Puckler superciliously.

No little girl has been seen, and he knew 'nothing about no dolls'.

'She is my little girl,' said Mr Puckler tremulously, for all his anxiety was returning tenfold, 'and I am afraid something has happened.'

The inferior person said rudely that 'nothing could have happened to her in that house, because she had not been there, which was a jolly good reason why'; and Mr Puckler was obliged to admit that the man ought to know, as it was his business to keep the door and let people in. He wished to be allowed to speak to the under nurse, who knew him; but the man was ruder than ever, and finally shut the door in his face.

When the doll doctor was alone in the street, he steadied himself by the railing, for he felt as though he were breaking in two, just as some dolls break, in the middle of the backbone.

Presently he knew that he must be doing something to find Else, and that gave him strength. He began to walk as quickly as he could through the streets, following every highway and byway which his little girl might have taken on her errand. He also asked several policemen in vain if they had seen her, and most of them answered him kindly, for they saw that he was a sober man and in his right senses, and some of them had little girls of their own.

It was one o'clock in the morning when he went up to his own door again, worn out and hopeless and brokenhearted. As he turned the key in the lock, his heart stood still, for he knew that he was awake and not dreaming, and that he really heard those tiny footsteps pattering to meet him inside the house along the passage.

But he was too unhappy to be much frightened any more, and his heart went on again with a dull regular pain, that found its way all through him with every pulse. So he went in, and hung up his hat in the dark, and found the matches in the cupboard and the candlestick in its place in the corner.

Mr Puckler was so much overcome and so completely worn out that he sat down in his chair before the worktable and almost fainted, as his face dropped forward upon his folded hands. Beside him the solitary candle burned steadily with a low flame in the still warm air.

'Else! Else!' he moaned against his yellow knuckles. And that was all he could say, and it was no relief to him. On the contrary, the very sound of the name was a new and sharp pain that pierced his ears and his head and his very soul. For every time he repeated the name it meant that little Else was dead, somewhere out in the streets of London in the dark.

He was so terribly hurt that he did not even feel something pulling gently at the skirt of his old coat, so gently that it was like the nibbling of a tiny mouse. He might have thought that it was really a mouse if he had noticed it.

'Else! Else!' he groaned, right against his hands.

Then a cool breath stirred his thin hair, and the low flame of the one candle dropped down almost to a mere spark, not flickering as though a draught were going to blow it out, but just dropping down as if it were tired out. Mr Puckler felt his hands stiffening with fright under his face; and there was a faint rustling sound, like some small silk thing blown in a gentle breeze. He sat up straight, stark and scared, and a small wooden voice spoke in the stillness.

'Pa-pa,' it said, with a break between the syllables.

Mr Puckler stood up in a single jump, and his chair fell over backwards with a smashing noise upon the wooden floor. The candle had almost gone out.

It was Nina's doll-voice that had spoken, and he should have known it among the voices of a hundred other dolls. And yet there was something more in it, a little human ring, with a pitiful cry and a call for help, and the wail of a hurt child. Mr Puckler stood up, stark and stiff, and tried to look round, but at first he could not, for he seemed to be frozen from head to foot.

Then he made a great effort, and he raised one hand to each of his temples, and pressed his own head round as he would have turned a doll's. The candle was burning so low that it might as well have been out altogether, for any light it gave, and the room seemed quite dark at first. Then he saw something. He would not have believed that he could be more frightened than he had been just before that. But he was, and his knees shook, for he saw the doll standing in the middle of the floor, shining with a faint and ghostly radiance, her beautiful glassy brown eyes fixed on his. And across her face the very thin line of the break he had mended shone as though it were drawn in light with a fine point of white flame.

Yet there was something more in the eyes, too: there was something human, like Else's own, but as if only the doll saw him through them, and not Else. And there was enough of Else to bring back all his pain and to make him forget his fear.

'Else! My little Else!' he cried aloud.

The small ghost moved, and its doll-arm slowly rose and fell with a stiff, mechanical motion.

'Pa-pa,' it said.

It seemed this time that there was even more of Else's tone echoing somewhere between the wooden notes that reached his ears so distinctly and yet so far away. Else was calling him, he was sure.

His face was perfectly white in the gloom, but his knees did not shake any more, and he felt that he was less frightened.

'Yes, child! But where? Where?' he asked. 'Where are you, Else!'

'Pa-pa!'

The syllables died away in the quiet room.

There was a low rustling of silk, the glassy brown eyes turned slowly away, and Mr Puckler heard the pitter-patter of the small feet in the bronze kid slippers as the figure ran straight to the door. Then the candle burned high again, the room was full of light, and he was alone.

Mr Puckler passed his hand over his eyes and looked about him. He could see everything quite clearly, and he felt that he must have been dreaming, though he was standing instead of sitting down, as he should have been if he had just waked up. The candle burned brightly now. There were the dolls to be mended, lying in a row with their toes up. The third one had lost her right shoe, and Else was making one. He knew that, and he was certainly not dreaming now. He had not been dreaming when he had come in from his fruitless search and had heard the doll's footsteps running to the door. He had not fallen asleep in his chair. How could he possibly have fallen asleep when his heart was breaking? He had been awake all the time.

He steadied himself, set the fallen chair upon its legs, and said to himself again very emphatically that he was a foolish old man. He ought to be out in the streets looking for his child, asking questions, and inquiring at the police stations, where all accidents were reported as soon as they were known, or at the hospitals.

'Pa-pa!'

The longing, wailing, pitiful little wooden cry rang from the

81

passage, outside the door, and Mr Puckler stood for an instant with white face, transfixed and rooted to the spot. A moment later his hand was on the latch. Then he was in the passage, with the light streaming from the open door behind him.

Quite at the other end he saw the little phantom shining clearly in the shadow, and the right hand seemed to beckon to him as the arm rose and fell once more. He knew all at once that it had not come to frighten him but to lead him, and when it disappeared, and he walked boldly towards the door, he knew that it was in the street outside, waiting for him. He forgot that he was tired and had eaten no supper, and had walked many miles, for a sudden hope ran through and through him, like a golden stream of life.

And sure enough, at the corner of the alley, and at the corner of the street, and out in Belgrave Square, he saw the small ghost flitting before him. Sometimes it was only a shadow, where there was other light, but then the glare of the lamps made a pale green sheen on its little Mother Hubbard frock of silk; and sometimes, where the streets were dark and silent, the whole figure shone out brightly, with its yellow curls and rosy neck. It seemed to trot along like a tiny child, and Mr Puckler could hear the pattering of the bronze kid slippers on the pavement as it ran. But it went very fast, and he could only just keep up with it, tearing along with his hat on the back of his head and his thin hair blown by the night breeze, and his horn-rimmed spectacles firmly set upon his broad nose.

On and on he went, and he had no idea where he was. He did not even care, for he knew certainly that he was going the right way.

Then at last, in a wide, quiet street, he was standing before a big, sober-looking door that had two lamps on each side of it, and a polished brass bell-handle, which he pulled.

And just inside, when the door was opened, in the bright light, there was the little shadow, and the pale green sheen of the little silk dress, and once more the small cry came to his ears, less pitiful, more longing.

'Pa-pa!'

The shadow turned suddenly bright, and out of the brightness the beautiful brown glass eyes were turned up happily to his, while the rosy mouth smiled so divinely that the phantom doll looked almost like a little angel just then.

'A little girl was brought in soon after ten o'clock,' said the quiet voice of the hospital doorkeeper. 'I think they thought she was only stunned. She was holding a big brown-paper box against her, and they could not get it out of her arms. She had a long plait of brown hair that hung down as they carried her.'

'She is my little girl,' said Mr Puckler, but he hardly heard his own voice.

He leaned over Else's face in the gentle light of the children's ward, and when he had stood there a minute the beautiful brown eyes opened and looked up to his.

'Pa-pa!' cried Else softly, 'I knew you would come!'

Then Mr Puckler did not know what he did or said for a moment, and what he felt was worth all the fear and terror and despair that had almost killed him that night. But by and by Else was telling her story, and the nurse let her speak, for there were only two other children in the room, who were getting well and were sound asleep.

'They were big boys with bad faces,' said Else, 'and they tried to get Nina away from me, but I held on and fought as well as I could till one of them hit me with something, and I don't remember any more, for I tumbled down and I suppose the boys ran away, and somebody found me there. But I'm afraid Nina is all smashed.'

'Here is the box,' said the nurse. 'We could not take it out of her arms till she came to herself. Would you like to see if the doll is broken?'

And she undid the string cleverly, but Nina was all smashed to pieces. Only the gentle light of the children's ward made a pale green sheen in the folds of the little Mother Hubbard frock.

The Fog Horn

RAY BRADBURY

Out there in the cold water, far from land, we waited every night for the coming of the fog, and it came, and we oiled the brass machinery and lit the fog light up in the stone tower. Feeling like two birds in the grey sky, McDunn and I sent the light touching out, red, then white, then red again, to eye the lonely ships. And if they did not see our light, then there was always our Voice, the great deep cry of our Fog Horn shuddering through the rags of mist to startle the gulls away like decks of scattered cards and make the waves turn high and foam.

'It's a lonely life, but you're used to it now, aren't you?' asked McDunn.

'Yes,' I said. 'You're a good talker, thank the Lord.'

'Well, it's your turn on land tomorrow,' he said, smiling, 'to dance the ladies and drink gin.'

'What do you think, McDunn, when I leave you out here alone?'

'On the mysteries of the sea.' McDunn lit his pipe. It was a quarter past seven of a cold November evening, the heat on, the light switching its tail in two hundred directions, the Fog Horn bumbling in the high throat of the tower. There wasn't a town for a hundred miles down the coast, just a road which came lonely through dead country to the sea, with few cars on it, a stretch of two miles of cold water out to our rock, and rare few ships.

'The mysteries of the sea,' said McDunn thoughtfully. 'You know, the ocean's the biggest damned snowflake ever? It rolls and swells a thousand shapes and colours, no two alike. Strange. One night, years ago, I was here alone, when all of the fish of the sea surfaced out there. Something made them swim in and lie in the bay, sort of trembling and staring up at the tower light going red, white, red, white across them so I could

see their funny eyes. I turned cold. They were like a big peacock's tail, moving out there until midnight. Then, without so much as a sound, they slipped away, the million of them was gone. I kind of think maybe, in some sort of way, they came all those miles to worship. Strange. But think how the tower must look to them, standing seventy feet above the water, the God-light flashing out from it, and the tower declaring itself with a monster voice. They never came back, those fish, but don't you think for a while they thought they were in the Presence?'

I shivered. I looked out at the long grey lawn of the sea stretching away into nothing and nowhere.

'Oh, the sea's full.' McDunn puffed his pipe nervously, blinking. He had been nervous all day and hadn't said why. 'For all our engines and so-called submarines, it'll be ten thousand centuries before we set foot on the real bottom of the sunken lands, in the fairy kingdoms there, and know *real* terror. Think of it, it's still the year 300,000 Before Christ down under there. While we've paraded around with trumpets, lopping each other's countries and heads, they have been living beneath the sea twelve miles deep and cold in a time as old as the beard of a comet.'

'Yes, it's an old world.'

'Come on. I got something special I been saving up to tell you.'

We ascended the eighty steps, talking and taking our time. At the top, McDunn switched off the room lights so there'd be no reflection in the plate glass. The great eye of the light was humming, turning easily in its oiled socket. The Fog Horn was blowing steadily, once every fifteen seconds.

'Sounds like an animal, don't it?' McDunn nodded to himself. 'A big lonely animal crying in the night. Sitting here on the edge of ten billion years calling out to the Deeps, I'm here, I'm here, I'm here. And the Deeps do answer, yes, they do. You been here now for three months, Johnny, so I better prepare you. About this time of year,' he said, studying the murk and fog, 'something comes to visit the lighthouse.'

'The swarms of fish like you said?'

'No, this is something else. I've put off telling you because you might think I'm daft. But tonight's the latest I can put it off, for if my calendar's marked right from last year, tonight's the night it comes. I won't go into detail, you'll have to see it yourself. Just sit down there. If you want, tomorrow you can pack your duffel and take the motorboat into land and get your car parked there at the dinghy pier on the cape and drive on back to some little inland town and keep your lights burning nights. I won't question or blame you. It's happened three years now, and this is the only time anyone's been here with me to verify it. You wait and watch.'

Half an hour passed with only a few whispers between us. When we grew tired waiting, McDunn began describing some of his ideas to me. He had some theories about the Fog Horn itself.

'One day many years ago a man walked along and stood in the sound of the ocean on a cold sunless shore and said, "We need a voice to call across the water, to warn ships; I'll make one. I'll make a voice like all of time and all of the fog that ever was; I'll make a voice that is like an empty bed beside you all night long, and like an empty house when you open the door, and like trees in autumn with no leaves. A sound like the birds flying south, crying, and a sound like November wind and the sea on the hard, cold shore. I'll make a sound that's so alone that no-one can miss it, that whoever hears it will weep in their souls, and hearths will seem warmer, and being inside will seem better to all who hear it in the distant towns. I'll make me a sound and an apparatus and they'll call it a Fog Horn and whoever hears it will know the sadness of eternity and the briefness of life." '

The Fog Horn blew.

'I made up that story,' said McDunn quietly, 'to try to explain why this thing keeps coming back to the lighthouse every year. The Fog Horn calls it, I think, and it comes . . .'

'But –' I said.

'Sssst!' said McDunn. 'There!' He nodded out to the Deeps. Something was swimming towards the lighthouse tower.

It was a cold night, as I have said; the high tower was cold, the light coming and going, and the Fog Horn calling and calling through the ravelling mist. You couldn't see far and you couldn't see plain, but there was the deep sea moving on its way about the night earth, flat and quiet, the colour of grey mud, and here were the two of us alone in the high tower, and there, far out at first, was a ripple, followed by a wave, a rising, a bubble, a bit of froth. And then, from the surface of the cold sea came a head, a large head, dark-coloured, with immense eyes, and then a neck. And then – not a body – but more neck and more! The head rose a full forty feet above the water on a slender and beautiful dark neck. Only then did the body, like a little island of black coral and shells and crayfish, drip up from the subterranean. There was a flicker of tail. In all, from head to tip of tail, I estimated the monster at ninety or a hundred feet.

I don't know what I said. I said something.

'Steady, boy, steady,' whispered McDunn.

'It's impossible!' I said.

'No, Johnny, *we're* impossible. *It's* like it always was ten million years ago. *It* hasn't changed. It's *us* and the land that've changed, become impossible. *Us!*'

It swam slowly and with a great dark majesty out in the icy waters, far away. The fog came and went about it, momentarily erasing its shape. One of the monster eyes caught and held and flashed back our immense light, red, white, red, white, like a disk held and sending a message in primeval code. It was as silent as the fog through which it swam.

'It's a dinosaur of some sort!' I crouched down, holding to the stair rail.

'Yes, one of the tribe.'

'But they died out!'

'No, only hid away in the Deeps. Deep, deep down in the deepest Deeps. Isn't *that* a word now, Johnny, a real word, it says so much: the Deeps. There's all the coldness and darkness and deepness in a word like that.'

'What'll we do?'

'Do? We got our job, we can't leave. Besides, we're safer here than in any boat trying to get to land. That thing's as big

88

as a destroyer and almost as swift.'

'But here, why does it come *here*?'

The next moment I had my answer.

The Fog Horn blew.

And the monster answered.

A cry came across a million years of water and mist. A cry so anguished and alone that it shuddered in my head and my body. The monster cried out at the tower. The Fog Horn blew. The monster roared again. The Fog Horn blew. The monster opened its great toothed mouth and the sound that came from it was the sound of the Fog Horn itself. Lonely and vast and far away. The sound of isolation, a viewless sea, a cold night, apartness. That was the sound.

'Now,' whispered McDunn, 'do you know why it comes here?'

I nodded.

'All year long, Johnny, that poor monster there lying far out, a thousand miles at sea, and twenty miles deep maybe, biding its time, perhaps it's a million years old, this one creature. Think of it, waiting a million years; could *you* wait that long? Maybe it's the last of its kind. I sort of think that's true. Anyway, here come men on land and build this light-house, five years ago. And set up their Fog Horn and sound it and sound it towards the place where you bury yourself in sleep and sea memories of a world where there were thousands like yourself, but now you're alone, all alone in a world not made for you, a world where you have to hide.

'But the sound of the Fog Horn comes and goes, comes and goes, and you stir from the muddy bottom of the Deeps, and your eyes open like the lenses of two-foot cameras and you move, slow, slow, for you have the ocean sea on your shoulders, heavy. But that Fog Horn comes through a thousand miles of water, faint and familiar, and the furnace in your belly stokes up, and you begin to rise, slow, slow. You feed yourself on great slakes of cod and minnow, on rivers of jellyfish, and you rise slow through the autumn months, through September when the fogs started, through October with more fog and the horn still calling you on, and then, late in November, after pressurizing yourself day by day, a few feet higher every hour, you are near the surface and still alive. You've got to go slow; if you surfaced all at once you'd explode. So it takes you all of three months to surface, and then a number of days to swim through the cold waters to the lighthouse. And there you are, out there, in the night, Johnny, the biggest damn monster in creation. And here's the lighthouse calling to you, with a long neck like your neck sticking way up out of the water, and a body like your body, and, most important of all, a voice like your voice. Do you understand now, Johnny, do you understand?'

The Fog Horn blew.

The monster answered.

I saw it all, I knew it all – the million years of waiting alone, for someone to come back who never came back. The million years of isolation at the bottom of the sea, the insanity of time there, while the skies cleared of reptile-birds, the swamps dried on the continental lands, the sloths and sabre-tooths had their day and sank in tar pits, and men ran like white ants upon the hills.

The Fog Horn blew.

'Last year,' said McDunn, 'that creature swam round and round, round and round, all night. Not coming too near, puzzled, I'd say. Afraid, maybe. And a bit angry after coming all this way. But the next day unexpectedly, the fog lifted, the sun came out fresh, the sky was as blue as a painting. And the monster swam off away from the heat and the silence and didn't come back. I suppose it's been brooding on it for a year now, thinking it over from every which way.'

The monster was only a hundred yards off now, it and the Fog Horn crying at each other. As the lights hit them, the monster's eyes were fire and ice, fire and ice.

'That's life for you,' said McDunn. 'Someone always waiting for someone who never comes home. Always someone loving some thing more than that thing loves them. And after a while you want to destroy whatever that thing is, so it can't hurt you no more.'

The monster was rushing at the lighthouse.

The Fog Horn blew.

'Let's see what happens,' said McDunn.

He switched the Fog Horn off.

The ensuing minute of silence was so intense that we could hear our hearts pounding in the glassed area of the tower, could hear the slow greased turn of the light.

The monster stopped and froze. Its great lantern eyes blinked. Its mouth gaped. It gave a sort of rumble, like a volcano. It twitched its head this way and that, as if to seek the sounds now dwindled off into the fog. It peered at the light-house. It rumbled again. Then its eyes caught fire. It reared up, threshed the water, and rushed at the tower, its eyes filled with angry torment.

'McDunn!' I cried. 'Switch on the horn!'

McDunn fumbled with the switch. But even as he flicked it on, the monster was rearing up. I had a glimpse of its gigantic paws, fishskin glittering in webs between the finger-like projections, clawing at the tower. The huge eye on the right side of its anguished head glittered before me like a cauldron into which I might drop, screaming. The tower shook. The Fog Horn cried; the monster cried. It seized the tower and gnashed at the glass, which shattered in upon us.

McDunn seized my arm. 'Downstairs!'

The tower rocked, trembled, and started to give. The Fog Horn and the monster roared. We stumbled and half fell down the stairs. 'Quick!'

We reached the bottom as the tower buckled down towards us. We ducked under the stairs into the small stone cellar. There were a thousand concussions as the rocks rained down; the Fog Horn stopped abruptly. The monster crashed upon the tower. The tower fell. We knelt together, McDunn and I, holding tight while our world exploded.

Then it was over, and there was nothing but darkness and the wash of the sea on the raw stones.

That and the other sound.

'Listen,' said McDunn quietly. 'Listen.'

We waited a moment. And then I began to hear it. First a great vacuumed sucking of air, and then the lament, the bewilderment, the loneliness of the great monster, folded over and upon us, above us, so that the sickening reek of its body filled the air, a stone's thickness away from our cellar. The monster gasped and cried. The tower was gone. The light was gone. The thing that had called to it across a million years was gone. And the monster was opening its mouth and sending out great sounds. The sounds of a Fog Horn, again and again. And ships far at sea, not finding the light, not seeing anything, but passing and hearing late that night, must've thought: There it is, the lonely sound, the Lonesome Bay horn. All's well. We've rounded the cape.

And so it went for the rest of that night.

The sun was hot and yellow the next afternoon when the rescuers came out to dig us from our stoned-under cellar.

'It fell apart, is all' said McDunn gravely. 'We had a few bad knocks from the waves and it just crumbled.' He pinched my arm.

There was nothing to see. The ocean was calm, the sky blue. The only thing was a great algaic stink from the green matter that covered the fallen tower stones and the shore rocks. Flies buzzed about. The ocean washed empty on the shore.

The next year they built a new lighthouse, but by that time I had a job in the little town and a wife and a good small warm house that glowed yellow on autumn nights, the doors locked, the chimney puffing smoke. As for McDunn, he was master of the new lighthouse, built to his own specifications, out of steel-reinforced concrete. 'Just in case,' he said.

The new lighthouse was ready in November. I drove down alone one evening late and parked my car and looked across the grey waters and listened to the new horn sounding, once, twice, three, four times a minute far out there, by itself.

The monster?

It never came back.

'It's gone away,' said McDunn. 'It's gone back to the Deeps. It's learned you can't love anything too much in this world. It's gone into the deepest Deeps to wait another million years. Ah, the poor thing! Waiting out there, and waiting out there, while man comes and goes on this pitiful little planet. Waiting and waiting.'

I sat in my car, listening. I couldn't see the lighthouse or the light standing out in Lonesome Bay. I could only hear the Horn, the Horn, the Horn. It sounded like the monster calling.

I sat there wishing there was something I could say.

S2 - Mrs Bergen.
Science -
Fiction
Unit .

Too long ?
perhaps :

Solo Talk: Assessment Sheets. 81/82.

Strand	Level B	Level C	Level D	Level E	Next Steps
Conveying information and instructions	Can convey a simple message with more than	Can organise a message with * brief report * straight-	Can convey info/instrs/ directions.	Can convey info/instrs/ directions. Displays:	

The Mouse

HOWARD FAST

Only the mouse watched the flying saucer descend to earth. The mouse crouched apprehensively in a mole's hole, its tiny nose twitching, its every nerve quivering in fear and attention as the beautiful golden thing made a landing.

The flying saucer – or circular spaceship, shaped roughly like a flattened, wide-brimmed hat – slid past the roof of the split-level suburban house, swam across the back yard, and then settled into a tangle of ramblers, nestling down among the branches and leaves so that it was covered entirely. And since the flying saucer was only about thirty inches in diameter and no more than seven inches in height, the camouflage was accomplished rather easily.

It was just past three o'clock in the morning. The inhabitants of this house and of all the other houses in this particular suburban development slept or tossed in their beds and struggled with insomnia. The passage of the flying saucer was soundless and without odour, so no dog barked; only the mouse watched – and he watched without comprehension, even as he always watched, even as his existence was – without comprehension.

What had just happened became vague and meaningless in the memory of the mouse – for he hardly had a memory at all. It might never have happened. Time went by, seconds, minutes, almost an hour, and then a light appeared in the tangle of briars and leaves where the saucer lay. The mouse fixed on the light, and then he saw two men appear, stepping out of the light, which was an opening into the saucer, and onto the ground.

Or at least they appeared to be vaguely like creatures the mouse had seen that actually were men – except that they were only three inches tall and enclosed in spacesuits. If the mouse

95

whiskered nose showing. The two men moved slowly and carefully, choosing their steps with great deliberation. One of them sank suddenly almost to his knees in a little bit of earth, and after that they attempted to find footing on stones, pebbles, bits of wood. Evidently their great weight made the hard, dry earth too soft for safety. Meanwhile the mouse watched them, and when their direction became evident, the mouse attempted the convulsive action of escape.

But his muscles would not respond, and as panic seared his small brain, the first spaceman reached into the mouse's mind, soothing him, finding the fear centre and blocking it off with his own thoughts and then electronically shifting the mouse's neuron paths to the pleasure centres of the tiny animal's brain. All this the spaceman did effortlessly and almost instantaneously, and the mouse relaxed, made squeaks of joy, and gave up any attempt to escape. The second spaceman then broke the dirt away from the tunnel mouth, lifted the mouse with ease, holding him in his arms and carried him back to the saucer. And the mouse lay there, relaxed and cooing with delight.

Two others, both women, were waiting in the saucer as the men came through the air lock, carrying the mouse. The women – evidently in tune with the men's thoughts – did not have to be told what had happened. They had prepared what could only be an operating table, a flat panel of bright light overhead and a board of instruments alongside. The light made a square of brilliance in the darkened interior of the spaceship.

'I am sterile,' the first woman informed the men, holding up hands encased in thin, transparent gloves, 'so we can proceed immediately.'

Like the men, the women's skin was yellow, not sallow but a bright, glowing lemon yellow, the hair rich orange. Out of the spacesuits, they would all be dressed more or less alike, barefoot and in shorts in the warm interior of the ship; nor did the women cover their well-formed breasts.

'I reached out,' the second woman told them. 'They're all asleep, but their minds!'

'We know,' the men agreed.

'I rooted around – like a journey through a sewer. But I picked up a good deal. The animal is called a mouse. It is symbolically the smallest and most harmless of creatures, vegetarian, and hunted by practically everything else on this curious planet. Only its size accounts for its survival, and its only skill is concealment.'

Meanwhile the two men had laid the mouse on the operating table, where it sprawled relaxed and squeaking contentment. While the men went to change out of their spacesuits, the second woman filled a hypodermic instrument, inserted the needle near the base of the mouse's tail, and gently forced the fluid in. The mouse relaxed and became unconscious. Then the two women changed the mouse's position, handling the – to them huge – animal with ease and dispatch, as if it had almost no weight; and actually in terms of the gravitation they were built to contend with, it had almost no weight at all.

When the two men returned, they were dressed as were the women, in shorts, and barefoot, with the same transparent gloves. The four of them then began to work together, quickly, expertly – evidently a team who had worked in this manner many times in the past. The mouse now lay upon its stomach, its feet spread. One man put a cone-shaped mask over its head and began the feeding of oxygen. The other man shaved the top of its head with an electric razor, while the two women began an operation which would remove the entire top of the mouse's skull. Working with great speed and skill, they incised the skin, and then using trephines that were armed with a sort of laser beam rather than a saw, they cut through the top of the skull, removed it, and handed it to one of the men who placed it in a pan that was filled with a glowing solution. The brain of the mouse was thus exposed.

The two women then wheeled over a machine with a turret top on a universal joint, lowered the top close to the exposed brain, and pressed a button. About a hundred tiny wires emerged from the turret top, and very fast, the women began to attach these wires to parts of the mouse's brain. The man who had been controlling the oxygen flow now brought over another machine, drew tubes out of it, and began a process of feeding fluid into the mouse's circulatory system, while the second man began to work on the skull section that was in the glowing solution.

The four of them worked steadily and apparently without fatigue. Outside, the night ended and the sun rose, and still the four space people worked on. At about noon, they finished the first part of their work and stood back from the table to observe and admire what they had done. The tiny brain of the mouse had been increased fivefold in size, and in shape and folds resembled a miniature human brain. Each of the four shared a feeling of great accomplishment, and they mingled their thoughts and praised each other and then proceeded to complete the operation. The shape of the skull section that had been removed was now compatible with the changed brain, and when they replaced it on the mouse's head, the only noticeable difference in the creature's appearance was a strange, high lump above his eyes. They sealed the breaks and joined the flesh with some sort of plastic, removed the tubes, inserted new tubes, and changed the deep unconciousness of the mouse to a deep sleep.

For the next five days the mouse slept – but from motionless sleep, its condition changed gradually, until on the fifth day it began to stir and move restlessly, and then on the sixth day it awakened. During those five days it was fed intravenously, massaged constantly, and probed constantly and telepathically. The four space people took turns at entering its mind and feeding it information, and neuron by neuron, section by section, they programmed its newly enlarged brain. They were very skilled at this. They gave the mouse background knowledge, understanding, language, and self-comprehension. They fed it a vast amount of information, balanced the information with a philosophical comprehension of the universe and its meaning, left it as it had been emotionally, without aggression or hostility, but also without fear. When the mouse finally awakened, it knew what it was and how it had become what it was. It still remained a mouse, but in the enchanting wonder and majesty of its mind, it was like no other mouse that had ever lived on the planet Earth.

The four space people stood around the mouse as it awakened and watched it. They were pleased, and since much in their nature, especially in their emotional responses, was childlike and direct, they could not help showing their pleasure and smiling at the mouse. Their thoughts were in the nature of a welcome, and all that the mind of the mouse could express was gratitude. The mouse came to its feet, stood on the floor where it had lain, faced each of them in turn, and then wept inwardly at the fact of its existence. Then the mouse was hungry and they gave it food. After that the mouse asked the basic, inevitable question:

'Why?'

'Because we need your help.'

'How can I help you when your own wisdom and power are apparently without measure?'

The first spaceman explained. They were explorers, cartographers, surveyors – and behind them, light-years away, was their home planet, a gigantic ball the size of our planet Jupiter. Thus their small size, their incredible density. Weighing on earth only a fraction of what they weighed at home, they nevertheless weighed more than any earth creature their size – so much more that they walked on earth in dire peril of sinking out of sight. It was quite true that they could go anywhere in their spacecraft, but to get all the information they required, they would have to leave it – they would have to venture forth on foot. Thus the mouse would be their eyes and their feet.

'And for this a mouse!' the mouse exclaimed. 'Why? I am the smallest, the most defenceless of creatures.'

'Not any longer,' they assured him. 'We ourselves carry no weapons, because we have our minds, and in that way your mind is like ours. You can enter the mind of any creature, a cat, a dog – even a man – stop the neuron paths to his hate and aggression centres, and you can do it all with the speed of thought. You have the strongest of all weapons – the ability to make any living thing love you, and having that, you need nothing else.'

Thus the mouse became part of the little group of space

people who measured, charted, and examined the planet Earth. The mouse raced through the streets of a hundred cities, slipped in and out of hundreds of buildings, crouched in corners where he was privy to the discussions of people of power who ruled this part or that part of the planet Earth, and the space people listened with his ears, smelled with his sensitive nostrils, and saw with his soft brown eyes. The mouse journeyed thousands of miles, across the seas and continents whose existence he had never dreamed about. He listened to professors lecture to auditoriums of college students, and he listened to the great symphony orchestras, the fine violinists and pianists. He watched mothers give birth to children and he listened to wars being planned and murders being plotted. He saw weeping mourners watch the dead interred in the earth, and he trembled to the crashing sounds of huge assembly lines in monstrous factories. He hugged the earth as bullets whistled overhead, and he saw men slaughter each other for reasons so obscure that in their own minds there was only hate and fear.

As much as the space people, he was a stranger to the curious ways of mankind, and he listened to them speculate on the mindless, haphazard mixture of joy and horror that was mankind's civilization on the planet Earth.

Then, when their mission was almost completed, the mouse chose to ask them about their own place. He was able to weigh facts now and to measure possibilities and to grapple with uncertainties and to create his own abstractions; and so he thought, on one of those evenings when the warmth of the five little creatures filled the spaceship, when they sat and mingled thoughts and reactions in an interlocking of body and mind of which the mouse was a part, about the place where they had been born.

'Is it very beautiful?' the mouse asked.

'It's a good place. Beautiful – and filled with music.'

'You have no wars?'

'No.'

'And no one kills for the pleasure of killing?'

'No.'

'And your animals – things like myself?'

'They exist in their own ecology. We don't disturb it, and we don't kill them. We grow and we make the food we eat.'

'And are there crimes like here – murder and assault and robbery?'

'Almost never.'

And so it went, question and answer, while the mouse lay there in front of them, his strangely shaped head between his paws, his eyes fixed on the two men and the two women with worship and love; and then it came as he asked them:

'Will I be allowed to live with you – with the four of you? Perhaps go on other missions with you? Your people are never cruel. You won't place me with the animals. You'll let me be with the people, won't you?'

They didn't answer. The mouse tried to reach into their minds, but he was still like a little child when it came to the game of telepathy, and their minds were shielded.

'Why?'

Still no response.

'Why?' he pleaded.

Then from one of the women. 'We were going to tell you. Not tonight, but soon. Now we must tell you. You can't come with us.'

'Why?'

'For the plainest of reasons, dear friend. We are going home.'

'Then let me go home with you. It's my home, too – the beginning of all my thoughts and dreams and hope.'

'We can't.'

'Why?' the mouse pleaded. 'Why?'

'Don't you understand? Our planet is the size of your planet Jupiter here in the solar system. That is why we're so small in earth terms – because our very atomic structure is different from yours. By the measure of weight they use here on earth, I weigh almost a hundred kilograms, and you weigh less than an eighth of a kilogram, and yet we are almost the same size. If we were to bring you to our planet, you would die the moment we reached its gravitational pull. You would be crushed so completely that all semblance of form in you would disappear. You can't ask us to destroy you.'

'But you are so wise,' the mouse protested. 'You can do almost anything. Change me. Make me like yourselves.'

'By your standards we are wise –' The space people were full of sadness. It permeated the room and the mouse felt its desolation. 'By our own standards we have precious little wisdom. We can't make you like us. That is beyond any power we might dream of. We can't even undo what we have done, and now we realize what we have done.'

'And what will you do with me?'

'The only thing we can do. Leave you here.'

'Oh, no.' The thought was a cry of agony.

'What else can we do?'

'Don't leave me here,' the mouse begged them. 'Anything – but don't leave me here. Let me make the journey with you, and then if I have to die I will die.'

'There is no journey as you see it,' they explained. 'Space is not an area for us. We can't make it comprehensible to you, only to tell you that it is an illusion. When we rise out of the earth's atmosphere, we slip into a fold of space and emerge in our own planetary system. So it would not be a journey that you would make with us – only a step to your death.'

'Then let me die with you,' the mouse pleaded.

'No – you ask us to kill you. We can't.'

'Yet you made me.'

'We changed you. We made you grow in a certain way.'

'Did I ask you to? Did you ask me whether I wanted to be like this?'

'God help us, we didn't.'

'Then what am I to do?'

'Live. That's all we can say. You must live.'

'How? How can I live? A mouse hides in the grass and knows only two things – fear and hunger. It doesn't even know that it is, and of the vast lunatic world that surrounds it, it knows nothing. But you gave me knowledge –'

'And we also gave you the means to defend yourself, so that you can live without fear.'

'Why? Why should I live? Don't you understand that?'

'Because life is good and beautiful – and in itself the answer to all things.'

'For me?' The mouse looked at them and begged them to look at him. 'What do you see? I am a mouse. In all the world there is no other creature like myself. Shall I go back to the mice?'

'Perhaps.'

'And discuss philosophy with them? And open my mind to them? Or should I have intercourse with those poor, damned mindless creatures? What am I to do? You are wise. Tell me. Shall I be the stallion of the mouse world? Shall I store up riches in roots and bulbs? Tell me, tell me,' he pleaded.

'We will talk about it again,' the space people said. 'Be with yourself for a while, and don't be afraid.'

Then the mouse lay with his head between his paws and he thought about the way things were. And when the space people asked him where he wanted to be, he told them:

'Where you found me.'

So once again the saucer settled by night into the back yard of the suburban split-level house. Once again the air lock opened, and this time a mouse emerged. The mouse stood there, and the saucer rose out of the swirling dead leaves and spun away, a fleck of gold losing itself in the night. And the mouse stood there, facing its own eternity.

A cat, awakened by the movement among the leaves, came towards the mouse and then halted a few inches away when the tiny animal did not flee. The cat reached out a paw, and then the paw stopped. The cat struggled for control of its own body and then it fled, and still the mouse stood motionless. Then the mouse smelled the air, oriented himself, and moved to the mouth of the old mole tunnel. From down below, from deep in the tunnel, came the warm, musky smell of mice. The mouse went down through the tunnel to the nest, where a male and a female mouse crouched, and the mouse probed into their minds and found fear and hunger.

The mouse ran from the tunnel up to the open air and stood there, sobbing and panting. He turned his head up to the sky and reached out with his mind – but what he tried to reach was already a hundred light-years away.

'Why? Why?' the mouse sobbed to himself. 'They are so good, so wise – why did they do this to me?'

He then moved toward the house. He had become an adept at entering houses, and only a steel vault would have defied him. He found his point of entry and slipped into the cellar of the house. His night vision was good, and this combined with his keen sense of smell enabled him to move swiftly and at will.

Moving through the shifting web of strong odours that marked any habitation of people, he isolated the sharp smell of old cheese, and he moved across the floor and under a staircase to where a mousetrap had been set. It was a primitive thing, a stirrup of hard wire bent back against the tension of a coil spring and held with a tiny latch. The bit of cheese was on the latch, and the slightest touch on the cheese would spring the trap.

Filled with pity for his own kind, their gentleness, their helplessness, their mindless hunger that led them into a trap so simple and unconcealed, the mouse felt a sudden sense of triumph, of ultimate knowledge. He knew now what the space people had known from the very beginning, that they had given him the ultimate gift of the universe – consciousness of his own being – and in the flash of that knowledge the mouse knew all things and knew that all things were encompassed in consciousness. He saw the wholeness of the world and of all the worlds that ever were or would be, and he was without fear or loneliness.

In the morning, the man of the split-level surburban house went down into his cellar and let out a whoop of delight.

'Got it,' he yelled up to his family. 'I got the little bastard now.'

But the man never really looked at anything, not at his wife, not at his kids, not at the world; and while he knew that the trap contained a dead mouse, he never even noticed that this mouse was somewhat different from the other mice. Instead, he went out to the back yard, swung the dead mouse by his tail, and sent it flying into his neighbour's back yard.

'That'll give him something to think about,' the man said, grinning.

Follow On

The Best Day of My Easter Holidays

About the Story

The story is written from the point of view of Ned back at school after being on holiday in Jamaica. It is imagined to be his response to that standard essay title much loved by some teachers 'The Best Day of My Holidays'. The comment at the end from the teacher indicates that he didn't think much of Ned's efforts. Through Ned's eyes, we see the flamboyant exuberant character of Jolly Jackson. We are also allowed to see the rather stuffy and straightlaced response of Ned's parents and can compare the two.

For Discussion or Writing

1. Why do the American tourists think it is funny when they are told that the Egertons are staying in Jamaica on Mr Egerton's fees?
2. What is the reaction of Mr Egerton to this? What does this suggest about his character, and what incidents later in the story bear this out?
3. Why does Mr Egerton obey Jolly Jackson and get in the back of the car?
4. Point out some of the things which Jolly Jackson says which prove to be wrong.
5. What does Ned mean when he says 'Jolly Jackson some-how made you say "Ooooooooooh"'?
6. Why does Mrs Egerton say 'Fortnum and Mason!'?
7. Do you think paying Jolly Jackson seven dollars was 'daylight robbery'? Or do you think the Egertons deserved to be taken advantage of? Explain.
8. Why, later, does Mrs Egerton worry about whether they have paid Jolly Jackson enough?
9. What does Ned feel about Jolly Jackson? Why?
10. How would you have felt if you had been Ned?

11. Are there any similarities in feelings and attitudes between Ned and Jolly Jackson?
12. Why do you think Ned's teacher gave him only B minus for his essay? How would you rate it?

For Writing
1. Write an account of the kind of person Jolly Jackson is and the kind of life he leads.
2. Contrast the characters and attitudes to life of Jolly Jackson and the Egertons.
3. Write a story about a holiday or an outing on which something comically disastrous occurs.
4. If you have visited an interesting place or a foreign country, write about it.

Further Reading
This story comes from a collection entitled *Black Faces, White Faces* which describes the impressions of a number of people on holiday in Jamaica. It was written for adults, but Jane Gardam has also written a number of novels for young readers. Here are some which you may like to try: *A Long Way from Verona*, *A Few Fair Days*, *The Summer After the Funeral* and *Bilgewater*.

The Loaded Dog

About the Story
This story tells of three prospectors searching for gold in the Australian outback. It was a hard and rough life. But there was also the companionship, the consolation of drink, and moments of hilarity as this story reveals.

For Discussion or Writing
1. What is your first impression of the dog? Why does this add to the comedy of what follows?
2. Describe Dave, Jim and Andy so as to bring out the differences in their personalities.
3. How seriously does the author take the injuries done to the dogs by the explosion? How can you explain this?

4. How do the bushmen react to the explosion?
5. Discuss why the story is humorous.

For Writing
1. Describe the events of the story from the point of view of the black retriever.
2. Write a story in which a dog wishing to be helpful in fact brings about chaos.
3. Write a story about a group of men prospecting for gold.
4. Write a story about the plan that goes wrong.

Further Reading
Henry Lawson was born in Australia in 1867 and died in 1922. He was well-known for his ballads, stories and sketches, mainly about the life and toil of prospectors, farmers and bushmen working in the wide and arid wastes of the Australian bush. His stories are full of dry humour and odd characters. If you enjoyed 'The Loaded Dog', read some more stories by Henry Lawson. Some have been collected in *The Humorous Stories of Henry Lawson* and in *The Bush Undertaker and Other Stories*.

To Build a Fire

About the Story
This story is set in the icy conditions of the Yukon. It is a simple story of man pitting himself against the elements, assuming that he is a superior being and that he can succeed. But Nature is stronger than he is. His companion, the dog, is more humble, realizes the dangers, and survives.

For Discussion or Writing
1. What sign is there in the very first paragraph that the man is not up to condition?
2. 'The trouble with him was that he was without imagination'. What does this mean, and how is this fact borne out by the rest of the story?
3. In what ways is the dog wiser than the man?
4. 'Any man who was a man could travel alone'. What does this tell us about the man? Detail how he is proved wrong.

5. What incident marks the beginning of the final disaster?
6. What does the man do as a final desperate effort to survive?
7. How does the man meet his death?
8. From this story, who is more able to withstand the forces of nature – the man or the dog? Why?
9. What aspects of the experience the man goes through would you find particularly unpleasant or distressing?
10. If you were the man, what would you have done in order to complete your journey safely?

For Writing
1. Write an account of the man's journey, making clear step by step how things go wrong.
2. Compare the dog in this story with the dog in 'The Loaded Dog'.
3. Write a story about someone who has to undertake a journey in difficult weather and how he succeeds or fails.
4. Imagine there is a severe winter and you and your family are snowed up in your house. Describe what you do.

Further Reading
Jack London was born in the United States of America in 1876 and died in 1916. He led a wild life in the course of which he worked in a canning factory, travelled as a sailor, went gold prospecting in the Klondyke, came to understand the feelings and hardships of working men, and made a fortune from his writing. The struggle of man against the elements of nature (particularly the sea and ice) constantly recurs in London's work. Try to read some more of his short stories. Novels by Jack London that you would enjoy are *The Call of the Wild* and *White Fang* which deal with the same kind of hard struggle described in 'To Build a Fire'.

Vaarlem and Tripp

About the Story
The story is set in the seventeenth century at the time of the sea wars between Holland and England and uses the tradition

of great artists like Vermeer, Rembrandt and Rubens as background. The story tells of a boy's views of his master, an artist, but the artist is not entirely contemptible, and the boy not entirely free from fault himself. The skill of the story lies in the way the author allows these facts to emerge from the story-teller's own words.

For Discussion or Writing

1. What are Roger Vaarlem's feelings about his master at the beginning of the story? Pick out the three qualities that Roger concentrates on. Is there another side to the picture?
2. What incidents in the story support Roger's view?
3. What aspects of his own character does Roger reveal by his opinion of his master?
4. Contrast the reactions of the three people in the boat to the sea battle.
5. What are their reactions to the wounding of Krebs?
6. Contrast the different feelings of Roger and his master on being captured by the English.
7. How does Tripp score an unexpected victory?
8. How does Roger feel about this?
9. A number of attitudes towards battle and war are indicated throughout the story. Pick them out and comment on them.
10. The author sometimes makes fun of Roger and his attitudes, though Roger himself hardly seems to be aware of this. Can you find examples?
11. What views on the value of a great artist are indicated in the story?
12. What is your opinion of Tripp?

For Writing

1. Write descriptions of Vaarlem and Tripp.
2. Write down your views on how important or valuable to society great artists and writers are.
3. Write a story in which someone who appears to be a coward saves the situation in the end.
4. Write a story in which a young character is constantly

embarrassed and shamed by the behaviour of an older character.

Further Reading

Leon Garfield is a very gifted writer of stories and novels for young readers. Most of his writing is set in the eighteenth century, but he is more interested in telling a story and revealing character and motive than he is in writing historical novels full of precise and accurate detail. He has an exuberant style and a lively sense of humour. If you enjoyed this story, you would enjoy the other stories in *Mister Corbett's Ghost* and in the series called *Garfield's Apprentices*. Novels by Leon Garfield you should try to read are *Jack Holborn*, *Black Jack*, *Smith*, *The Devil-in-the-Fog*, *The Drummer Boy* and *The Strange Affair of Adelaide Harris*.

The Body-Snatcher

About the Story

The story begins in the middle of the nineteenth century but looks back to the time in Edinburgh nearer the beginning of the century when Burke and Hare were notorious for digging up dead bodies in order to supply the medical schools with bodies for their students to dissect. When there were not enough natural deaths, other means were used to ensure that the supply of bodies continued. It is an eerie tale of the supernatural, but it also uses the supernatural to show up the difference between one man and another, to show how the same event can affect consciences in different ways.

For Discussion or Writing

1. What kind of atmosphere does the opening paragraph create? What is the relevance of this to the rest of the story?
2. Contrast the appearance of Fettes and Dr Macfarlane.
3. Describe the encounter between Fettes and Dr Macfarlane at the George.
4. What was Fettes' position as a student?

5. What was Mr K's attitude towards his supply of corpses for anatomy?
6. What is the significance of the fact that Fettes recognises one of the bodies as being that of Jane Galbraith?
7. What impression do we get of Wolfe Macfarlane as a young man?
8. What is Macfarlane's attitude towards the body of Jane Galbraith?
9. When we first meet Gray, what seems to be his relationship with Macfarlane?
10. What do you think the hold is that Gray has over Macfarlane?
11. Whose body does Macfarlane bring to Fettes?
12. Why does Macfarlane insist on being paid for it?
13. What hold does Macfarlane have over Fettes?
14. Why does Macfarlane's sale of Gray's body to Fettes seem a perfect way of concealing his crime?
15. Who was 'the Resurrection Man'?
16. How does the weather add to the atmosphere of the journey of Fettes and Macfarlane to dig up the body in Glencorse?
17. How can you explain the change that takes place in the body?
18. From what we learn at the beginning of the story, what effect does this experience have on Fettes and on Macfarlane?

For Writing

1. Imagine that you are interviewing Fettes or Macfarlane about those events in Edinburgh and write down what he says.
2. Write a story which tells how Jane Galbraith died.
3. Write a story about a visit late at night to a graveyard.
4. Write a supernatural story about someone who is troubled by a bad conscience.

Further Reading

Robert Louis Stevenson was born in Edinburgh in 1850 and died in Samoa in 1894. He travelled much, particularly in the South Seas, where he finally settled because of his poor health.

He was a born story-teller. If you enjoyed this story, try to read some of these other stories by him: 'The Bottle Imp', 'Thrawn Janet', 'Markheim', 'The Sire de Malétroit's Door' and 'The Beach of Falesá'. Well-known novels by Stevenson you would enjoy are *Treasure Island*, *Kidnapped*, *The Strange Case of Dr Jekyll and Mr Hyde*, *The Master of Ballantrae* and *The Weir of Hermiston* (which was left unfinished).

The Doll's Ghost

About the Story

This is a very simply told story, set in Victorian London, about a doll doctor's love for the dolls he cares for and for his daughter, and how these two loves come together to relieve his anxiety and worry. Although, on the surface, it appears to be a story of the supernatural, it could also have a more naturalistic explanation. Some readers may find the story sentimental, but the simple language with which it is told and the contrast betwen Mr Puckler and his daughter and the people at Cranston House help to give the story genuine feeling.

For Discussion or Writing

1. How is the accident to the doll made to seem a terrible accident?
2. Why do the nurses want to keep the accident quiet?
3. Can you describe the difference in attitude of the author towards the goings-on at Cranston House and his attitude towards Mr Puckler and his daughter?
4. Describe Mr Puckler and his circumstances.
5. How does Mr Puckler's treatment of the doll Nina almost lead us to believe that she is alive?
6. Why does Mr Puckler begin to worry about Else?
7. What signs are there that he is beginning to get upset?
8. How does Mr Puckler's reception at Cranston House recall the opening paragraphs of the story?
9. How could you explain that Mr Puckler's state prepares him to be ready to hear the doll?
10. How would you explain the doll's ghost?
11. Do you think there is any connection between Mr Puckler's

feelings for his dolls and the way in which the doll helps
him to find his daughter again?

For Writing
1. Tell the story from Else's point of view.
2. Write a story about a doll that comes alive.
3. You are walking along the street late at night when you hear
   footsteps coming behind you. Describe what happens next.

Further Reading
F. Marion Crawford was born in Italy in 1854, the son of an
American sculptor. He died in 1919. His first novel, *Mr Isaacs*,
was a great success, and he followed it with forty others, mainly
historical romances. His books, however, are not much read
nowadays.

The Fog Horn

About the Story
This story puts man in his place. We don't know everything
about the universe, and there may be beneath the sea creatures
who have lived longer and suffered more than we have. The
author creates the suspense of the two men in the lighthouse
waiting for the coming of the monster, but also sympathy for
this lonely creature who is bewildered and dispossessed.

For Discussion or Writing
1. What factors in the opening of the story create a strange
   and mysterious atmosphere?
2. In what ways is the fog horn like a god and in what ways is
   it like an animal?
3. What emotion does McDunn feel that the fog horn's call
   embodies?
4. Why does the monster come to the fog horn?
5. What human parallel does McDunn make to the monster
   and the fog horn?
6. What are your feelings about the monster's visit?
7. Why does the monster roar with grief when the lighthouse
   is destroyed?

8. Why do you think McDunn gives the explanation he does give for the destruction of the lighthouse?
9. What are the narrator's feelings at the end of the story?
10. Do you think this story could happen?

For Writing
1. Write about what a day in the life of a lighthouse-keeper must be like.
2. Write another story about a monster that rises unexpectedly from the deep.
3. Imagine you were the last man or woman left on earth. Describe what you feel.

Further Reading
Ray Bradbury is an American science fiction writer, though many of his stories are fantasy (like 'The Fog Horn') rather than stories about the future. Although his stories are usually about strange and impossible events, the way in which they are told makes us believe them and also makes us think more seriously about the kind of world in which we live. If you enjoyed 'The Fog Horn', try to read some more stories by Ray Bradbury. Collections of them include *The October Country*, *The Illustrated Man*, *The Golden Apples of the Sun* and *The Day It Rained Forever*. Older readers may also enjoy the novel *Fahrenheit 451* which describes a society where books are forbidden and burned.

The Mouse

About the Story
This is another science fiction story in which the author imagines a tiny spaceship coming to earth and transforming the brain of a mouse so that the mouse can feed back information about what the earth is like. Science fiction stories often describe fantastic worlds or describe events that couldn't possibly happen. But while we read, we believe what the writer tells us, and often the stories can give us an insight into the actual world we live in. This story is of that kind.

For Discussion or Writing
1. Why is the mouse shown at the beginning of the story as barely comprehending what is going on when the spaceship arrives?
2. What impression do the telepaths get of human beings?
3. Explain how the spacemen capture the mouse.
4. Why do the telepaths transform the mouse?
5. Why do the telepaths and the mouse not require any weapons?
6. What are the differences between society on earth and society on the telepaths' planet?
7. Why can't the mouse go home with the telepaths?
8. Why does the mouse want to go with them?
9. What are the mouse's thoughts when he finds the mouse-trap?
10. What impression do you get of the man in the final section of the story? What relevance does this have to the rest of the story?
11. What point do you think the author is trying to make in this story?

For Writing
1. Write a story describing one of the adventures the mouse has as it explores the earth.
2. Write the report the telepaths make when they arrive back home.
3. Write a story about visitors from another planet arriving on earth.
4. Write a story about an animal, perhaps a pet, which suddenly starts behaving rather oddly. . . .

Further Reading
Howard Fast was born in New York in 1914. He writes mainly historical novels and shows great concern for the working man and his struggle. His best-known novel is *Spartacus* which describes how Spartacus led the slaves' revolt against their Roman masters.

For Discussion or Writing

1. Why is the mouse shown at the beginning of the story as barely comprehending what is going on when the spaceship arrives?
2. What impression do the telepaths get of human beings?
3. Explain how the spacemen capture the mouse.
4. Why do the telepaths transform the mouse?
5. Why do the telepaths and the mouse not require any weapons?
6. What are the differences between society on earth and society on the telepaths' planet?
7. Why can't the mouse go home with the telepaths?
8. Why does the mouse want to go with them?
9. What are the mouse's thoughts when he finds the mouse-trap?
10. What impression do you get of the man in the final section of the story? What relevance does this have to the rest of the story?
11. What point do you think the author is trying to make in this story?

For Writing

1. Write a story describing one of the adventures the mouse has as it explores the earth.
2. Write the report the telepaths make when they arrive back home.
3. Write a story about visitors from another planet arriving on earth.
4. Write a story about an animal – perhaps a pet – which suddenly starts behaving rather oddly.

Further Reading
Howard Fast was born in New York in 1914. He writes mainly historical novels and shows great concern for the working man and his struggle. His best-known novel is Spartacus which describes how Spartacus led the slaves' revolt against their Roman masters.